Tad's Treasure

(Baker City Brides Prequel)
A Sweet Historical Western Romance
by
USA Today Bestselling Author
SHANNA HATFIELD

[handwritten inscription] To Diane — Happy Reading! Shanna Hatfield 6/17

Tad's Treasure

ISBN-13: 978-1542717144
ISBN-10: 1542717140

To Mom -
For all the memories
stitched with love...

Books by Shanna Hatfield

FICTION

CONTEMPORARY

Love at the 20-Yard Line
The Coffee Girl
The Christmas Crusade
Learnin' the Ropes
QR Code Killer

Rodeo Romance Series
The Christmas Cowboy
Wrestlin' Christmas
Capturing Christmas
Barreling Through Christmas

Grass Valley Cowboys Series
The Cowboy's Christmas Plan
The Cowboy's Spring Romance
The Cowboy's Summer Love
The Cowboy's Autumn Fall
The Cowboy's New Heart
The Cowboy's Last Goodbye

Women of Tenacity Series
A Prelude
Heart of Clay
Country Boy vs. City Girl
Not His Type

HISTORICAL

Hardman Holidays
The Christmas Bargain
The Christmas Token
The Christmas Calamity
The Christmas Vow
The Christmas Quandary

Pendleton Petticoats Series
Dacey
Aundy
Caterina
Ilsa
Marnie
Lacy
Bertie
Millie

Baker City Brides
Tad's Treasure
Crumpets and Cowpies
Thimbles and Thistles
Corsets and Cuffs

Hearts of the War
Garden of Her Heart

NON-FICTION

Fifty Dates with Captain Cavedweller
Farm Girl
Recipes of Love

Savvy Entertaining Series

Chapter One

1886
Baker City, Oregon

A familiar aroma filled Tad Palmer's workshop as he skillfully guided a knife through a piece of thick leather.

The scent of the tanned hide took his thoughts back to childhood summers spent on his family's ranch in Kansas with a crusty old cowboy named Butch. Thanks to the man's patient instruction, Tad had learned how to turn leather into saddles known as some of the best in the region.

As he worked to trim the leather that would eventually line the seat of a stock saddle one of the local ranchers ordered, the bell above his shop door jingled with a cheerful sound of welcome.

"Be right there," Tad called as the door clicked shut and the bell quieted. He set aside the knife and hurried through the curtain-covered doorway into the front of his saddle shop. The sight of the man moving down the double row of saddles on display made him smile and stride forward with his hand held out in friendly greeting. "What's an ugly ol' cuss like you doing out this early in the day?"

John Jacobs took his hand and gave it a hearty shake. "Who are you calling an ugly cuss, you cranky ol' hound? I can't be too awful bad or I wouldn't have such a pretty little wife and son."

Tad grinned and slapped his friend on the back. "You've got that right, I suppose." He walked over to the stove and used a folded polishing cloth to lift a pot of coffee, filling two cups. After he handed one to John, he took a sip. "What brings you by this morning?"

John leaned back against the long, polished wooden counter that stood in front of shelves stocked with gloves, oil, bits, and spurs. He took a deep swig of his coffee and grimaced. One eye squeezed shut, as though he tried to reconcile his tastebuds to what he'd just swallowed. "How long has that been percolating?"

"Not that long." Tad took another drink just to prove the coffee was passable. "Not all of us have an adoring wife to fetch our slippers, make us coffee, and treat us like a king."

John grinned. "Not all women are like my Posey. She's one of a kind."

"Agreed," Tad said, then nudged John with his elbow. "Then again, I plan to remain single my whole life. I've long ago gotten used to drinking my coffee."

"It's an acquired taste, Tad, and one I don't plan to ever acquire," John teased, then sobered. "Posey and I keep hoping one of these days we'll talk some sense into that thick skull of yours and get you to realize not all women are evil and conniving. Just because your…"

"What can I do for you, John?" Tad asked, cutting him off. The last thing he wanted to do was think about hurts from what seemed like a lifetime ago. Pain that should remain buried.

John motioned toward the front window with his cup. "I have a load of blasting supplies arriving on the train today. I was hoping I could convince my mining partner to haul it up to the mine for me. I don't trust anyone but you to haul the explosives."

Tad nodded. "I reckon I could take care of it, as long as you remember my partnership in The Limitless remains silent."

John shrugged. "It makes no difference to me, but I don't know why it matters so much to you."

"I just want to focus on building up my saddle shop, not on mining. You know you have my support, but I don't want to be involved in the day to day running of the mine."

"I know, partner." John grinned at him. "Don't you miss the good old days when we first arrived in town, all as green as new grass?"

Tad laughed. "No, I do not miss those days. And I'm sure Posey doesn't either. We lived in tents and hardly had two nickels to rub together. It's a good thing the mine we went to work for paid well. I told you as soon as I earned enough I was opening my shop."

"And you did." John looked around the tidy store redolent with the scents of leather and oil. "We've come a long way in the last six years, haven't we?"

"We sure have," Tad agreed, refilling his coffee cup. "You and Posey have a nice house and little Nathaniel, and own a potentially prosperous mine."

"Partly own an almost prosperous mine. The other half is all yours." John finished the last of his coffee and set the cup on the counter. "You know as well as I do I couldn't have purchased the mine without your help. The hours and hours of free labor you contributed when I was getting started made all the difference in the world. Posey and I both owe you a big debt."

"You would have done the same for me. In fact, you helped me hang every shelf in here and I'm certain your wife charmed half the men in town into coming to purchase something whether they needed it or not when I first opened."

John beamed with pride. "That's my girl. All she has to do is smile and no one can tell her no."

"That's what I'm talking about, John. You are whipped, and you like it."

John laughed. "I certainly do." He thumped Tad on the back as they moseyed toward the door. "Will it be any trouble to bring the supplies up later?"

"Not at all. I'll load them right off the train and bring them up. I can get someone to watch the shop for me for a few hours. Mr. Bentley is always looking for a few extra dollars and it's too early in the year for the city to pay him to drive the sprinkler wagon over the streets."

"That fusty old geezer probably runs off more customers than he helps," John said, opening the door, allowing a waft of fresh spring air to blow inside.

Tad chuckled. "Probably, but it makes him feel needed."

John settled his hat more firmly on his head then looked at Tad. "Despite what anyone might say, you're just a big-hearted fool. You know that?"

"So you've told me, more than once. Now get out of here. One of us has a bunch of work to finish before he has to traipse into the mountains with a wagon full of explosives."

"If you didn't want the job of handling transportation of The Limitless Mine's explosives, you shouldn't be so good at doing it."

Tad snorted. "The alternative to being good at doing it would mean I'd either be maimed or dead, you idiot."

John chuckled and jogged toward the horse he'd left tied down the street. "I'll see you later."

Tad waved a hand then stepped inside his shop. Since the early spring morning still carried a nip in the air, he closed the door then returned to his workshop.

Hours later, he straightened and rolled his shoulders to loosen muscles tightened from bending over and stamping an intricate pattern into leather. Pleased with the progress he made on the saddle, he rubbed his thumb over the design of the left skirt.

One of the first saddles he'd ever made held a similar pattern. Butch had praised his efforts, telling him he had a natural talent for making saddles that were both a thing of beauty and well crafted. He'd been so proud when he returned home to Virginia with the saddle. The recipient of his precious gift had laughed at him before demanding he get such a ridiculous thing out of her sight.

Before his memories swamped him, a whistle blew, alerting anyone listening to the arrival of the train.

Tad set aside his tools, locked the shop's back door, and then walked out front. Mr. Bentley had already committed himself to helping one of the widows in town repair a section of fence around her yard, so Tad decided just to lock his shop while he was at the mine. He'd stepped outside and started to turn the key in the lock when Posey Jacobs scurried around the corner. She held a baby on one arm while a heavy basket dangled from her other hand

"What are you doing here?" Tad asked. He took the basket from her hand and then bent down to make a silly face at the infant.

She smiled as the baby flapped a hand at him in recognition and jabbered excitedly. Tad spent more time than he thought he should eating dinner at the Jacobs' table. He adored little Nate and held him every chance he got. With no plans to have children of his own, he figured he'd have to enjoy John's offspring to make up for it.

"John forgot his lunch this morning, so I thought perhaps you could take it to him. There's plenty for you both." Posey tipped her head toward the store behind them. "I didn't know if you had someone to watch the shop, so Nate and I can stay until you get back."

"That's okay, Posey. It won't kill my business to be closed for a few hours in the middle of the day."

Posey shook her head and turned the key in the lock, unlocking the door before handing the key back to Tad. "We'll be perfectly fine."

"But, there are a lot of sharp tools, knives, and…" Tad started to worry about Nate getting hurt. Or Posey. John would kill him if anything happened to either of them.

Much to his surprise, she gave him a push with her free hand. "Go on, Tad. It's not like Nate can get into your tools and I'll certainly leave them alone." A teasing grin lit her face. "However, I might do some cleaning in there. When was the last time you washed your windows?"

"Suit yourself." Tad backed up a few paces, knowing he needed to get to the train. "I'll hurry."

"Take your time, Tad. It does you good to get outside in the fresh air and it's such a lovely spring day today."

"It is at that, Posey. I'll see you two in a while." Tad tipped his hat to her then rushed off in the direction of the train depot. He'd paid one of the boys who stopped by his shop earlier to run over to the livery to get his team and wagon, and then drive them to the depot.

Easily finding his wagon waiting alongside several others near the train tracks, Tad set the basket of food beneath the seat, checked the harnesses, and then climbed up to the tall seat. He backed the wagon into place in front of one of the train cars and carefully loaded the explosives.

After steadfastly tying the load with rope so it couldn't jostle, he drove away from the train station and followed the road leading out of town into the mountains. About halfway up the road, he veered left and followed another road for a few miles. He turned right and guided the horses along a narrow trail for another mile before he arrived at the road to The Limitless.

All was quiet as he tugged on the reins, pulling the horses to a stop outside the mine. "John?" He listened, wondering where the man could be. Most likely he was deep in the mine, working away.

Rather than go in search for him, Tad got busy unloading the supplies, using a key from a ring in his pocket to open the padlock on a storage shed where John kept the explosives. With sure, steady movements, Tad unloaded the wagon and then locked the shed.

"John?" he called again, moving toward the opening of the mine. Tad had hated the long, dark hours spent in mines when he worked beside John. But they'd both needed money to pursue their dreams, so he'd forced himself not to dwell on the cold, dank blackness around him and did his job until he saved enough to open his saddle shop.

It had been more than a year since he'd opened it and almost a year since he'd become John's silent partner in the mine.

"Are you in here, John?" Tad called, stepping inside the mine, squinting into the inky tunnel ahead of him.

A faint moan reached his ears and sent him into action. He lit a candle in a holder John kept near the door and hurried into the mine. He followed the curve of the tunnel and sucked in a gulp when he saw John pinned against the wall by a collapsed timber. The jagged edge of the wood had pierced his chest.

"Oh, John," Tad said, holding up the candle, trying to assess what could be done for his friend. He shoved the candleholder into a rock shelf jutting out at eye level and frantically tried to lift the heavy timber from his friend.

"Tad?" John's voice sounded weak when he spoke.

"Yeah, it's me." Determined to move the timber but afraid of what it would do to John when he did, Tad scrambled to clear away rock piled around the man's unmoving form. "If this is your way of getting out of unloading the wagon, I'd have to say it's a little extreme, even for you."

A noise, something between a laugh and cough, tore from John's throat then the man turned his glazed gaze on his friend.

Eyes wide, Tad noticed blood trickling from John's mouth. He reached for his handkerchief to wipe it away, but John shook his head.

"Don't bother," John rasped, weakly lifting his hand to grasp Tad's wrist. He took a ragged, wheezing breath. "Promise me?"

"Anything, John. You know I'd do anything for you." Tad would have promised the moon at that moment if John had asked for it then found a way to reel it down to him.

"Take care of Posey and Nate. They'll need you." John wheezed again as his grip tightened on Tad's wrist. "Promise? Take care of them."

"I will, John. You know I will, but let's concentrate on getting you out of here and down the hill to Doc. He'll have you fixed up in no time."

Slowly, John's head shifted back and forth. "Not this time, Tad." He coughed, blood flowing from the corner of his mouth. "Thanks for being a good friend."

"Thank you, John, for being a good friend and closer than a brother." Tad blinked away the moisture gathering in his eyes and wrapped his arms around the timber. With savage, brute force fueled by desperation, he yanked it away from John.

A sickening gurgle emanated from his friend's chest, but Tad ignored it. He lifted John and carried him out to the wagon. Quickly covering him with his coat, Tad leaped up to the seat and drove his team as fast as he dared into town.

By the time he arrived at the doctor's office, a small crowd gathered around him. "Someone get Posey. She's watching my shop," he said, lifting John's shoulders as one of the men in the crowd stepped forward and took the limp legs in his hands.

John opened his eyes as they laid him on a table in the doctor's examination room. His skin had taken on an ashen hue and his breath came in great gasps. He looked to Tad one final time, silently pleading with him to bend down.

Tad bent over until his ear was close to John's mouth. "Treasure my girl, Tad. Take care of her and Nate."

"John, I..." At the unmistakable look on his friend's face, Tad merely nodded, fighting back the tears that stung his eyes. "Partner, I don't want things to end like this."

John blinked twice then closed his eyes. He drew his last breath as the door burst open and Posey rushed inside.

"John? John!" she screamed.

Tad stepped in front of her, blocking the gruesome sight of her husband and wrapping the woman in his arms. He could hear Nate fussing from the front office where he'd been unceremoniously left with someone.

"Everything will be fine, Posey. I promise."

Even as he said the words, Tad had no idea how he'd make them come true.

Chapter Two

1890

Tad took a deep breath, inhaling the fresh spring air wafting in his workshop window as it blended with the scents of his saddle-making trade.

Even after years of working with leather, he never tired of the smell or the supple feel of it in his hands.

As he guided his knife along the line of the pattern he'd drawn to cut out the cantle of a saddle, he wondered if the coffee he'd put on had heated yet.

He set aside his knife and wandered into the front of his shop. After pouring a cup of the steaming brew, he took a long sip, pleased that his ability to make coffee had vastly improved over the years. In fact, a few of the old timers liked to drink coffee and flap their gums as they perched in chairs around his stove when it was too cold for them to sit in front of the general store and play checkers.

Tad took another swig of the coffee then turned and stared out the front window.

For all appearances, it looked like another peaceful spring day in Baker City. He stepped closer to the window and gazed across the street, noticing Posey Jacobs' wagon parked there, although the woman was nowhere in sight.

A frown burrowed into Tad's brow as he wondered if she'd taken Nate along with her. The little boy was a handful on a good day, but she always brought him with her to town. Most women who'd taken a turn keeping an eye on the rascal rarely did it more than once or twice. To give Posey a few moments of peace, Tad often watched Nate at his shop while she hurried to the mercantile, post office, or took care of other errands.

He was about to turn back to his work when movement down the street caught his eye. He watched as Nate swished a tin cup in a watering trough then carried the vessel full of water over to a spot where he'd created a mud puddle. The little boy hunkered down and stirred the water into the dirt, creating an awful mess.

Since he wasn't bothering anyone, though, or into trouble, Tad decided to leave him be. He sipped his coffee and watched as Nate carried over a few more cups of water. The boy used his teeth to tug up his shirtsleeves to keep them out of the mud before he started working it again.

The youngster formed what appeared to be a mud pie, tamping it into a bent tin pie plate. Tad wondered where Nate had acquired the tin kitchen pieces, but the boy could have found them most anywhere.

Nate carried the pie tin over to a set of finely tooled saddlebags draped over the hitching rail outside one of the saloons. Tad knew the saddlebags were well made because he'd been the one to craft them.

Before he could holler at the boy to stop, Nate opened one side of the saddlebag and slid the pie tin inside.

Tad clunked his coffee cup down on the counter, yanked the front door open, and jogged across the street. Unfortunately, Joe Lambery, the owner of the saddlebags, rushed out of the saloon, bellowing at Nate to get away from his things before Tad reached the boy.

While most children might cower in fear, Nate simply glanced up at the infuriated man with an impish grin.

"Gee, mister, I just thought ya might like a mud pie. My mama always likes it when I make them for her." Nate proudly handed the man the muddy tin cup in his hand.

"Why, I ought to…"

Tad stepped in front of Nate and put a restraining hand on Joe's arm as he raised a fist toward the boy.

Most people thought twice before entering a scuffle with Tad. Despite a peaceable demeanor, his quiet strength and broad shoulders made him a formidable foe if someone riled his temper.

"Mr. Lambery, the boy didn't mean anything by it," Tad said, clamping a hand over Nate's shoulder before he could scamper away.

"I don't care! That little devil just ruined my new saddlebags! You know they were expensive, since you made 'em. I spent all winter freezing my toes off up in the hills to make ends meet and that little monster made a mess of something that cost me dearly." Joe made a grab for Nate, but Tad stepped between them.

Tad had to work to hold back a laugh when Nate leaned around him and stuck out his tongue at Joe. What Nate had done was wrong, but Joe Lambery was a lazy, shiftless saddle tramp who did as little as possible to get by. He never worked more than a week or two at any one place. Tad wasn't certain the man wasn't involved in some illegal schemes because he'd disappear for a while then return to Baker City with his pockets full of money.

Joe would buy himself new clothes then waste the rest on booze and women. When Joe had appeared in town a month ago, he'd ordered the saddlebags. Tad had just finished them the previous afternoon, so it was a shame for Nate to fill them with mud pies, even if Joe probably deserved it.

"Look, Joe, the boy didn't mean any harm. He was just playing. You know how kids are."

The infuriated man shook his head. "I don't know how kids are. If this one is a representative of how they all behave, I ain't got no inclination to ever discover how they truly are!" Joe's face reddened and he made another grab for Nate.

Tad easily blocked him while keeping a grip on the child's arm. He shifted his gaze from Joe to the boy, pinning Nate with a warning glare. Nate stopped squirming around and stood still.

"Now, Joe, if Nate were to clean out your saddlebags, do you think...

"What's going on here?" Posey Jacobs asked as she waded into the throng of men surrounding Tad,

Joe, and her son. The men gathered around all doffed their hats and politely tipped their heads to her.

"Your little hooligan ruined my brand-new saddlebags. That's what's going on." Joe waggled an accusing finger at Nate as the boy cowered behind Tad. "He filled them full of mud!"

"I'm terribly sorry, sir," Posey said contritely. She glanced at Tad and he offered her a barely perceptible nod, letting her know Joe spoke the truth.

She grabbed Nate's hand and pulled him beside her. "Young man, I believe you have some explaining to do. Why did you fill Mr. Lambery's saddlebags with mud?"

"I didn't fill them with mud, Mama. I made him a mud pie. He had a pie tin and everything," Nate said, as though that adequately explained his actions.

"Nate," Posey cupped his chin in her hand and forced him to meet her gaze. "What have I told you about touching things that don't belong to you?"

"Not to, but, Mama..."

"No, excuses, young man." Posey gave him a stern look. "You will apologize to Mr. Lambery and then you'll clean out his saddlebags." She glanced at Tad. "They can be cleaned, can't they?"

"They sure can. I'll take them back to my shop and help Nate," Tad said, lifting the saddlebags. He tipped them over and soupy mud oozed out.

Joe glared at the boy, not amused or appeased.

Posey hurried over to her wagon and lifted a biscuit tin from a basket in the back. She returned and handed it to Joe. "Perhaps this will help smooth things over?"

Joe worked the lid off the tin and the scent of baked goods filled the air. He lifted a cookie and took a bite, appreciation evident on his face as he hurriedly ate that one and took another. "I reckon, Mrs. Jacobs, if your boy will clean out my saddlebags so that they look as good as new, I can forget this incident. But if he ever does it again, I'll string him up by his toes and leave him hanging from a tree in the desert for buzzard bait."

Nate's eyes widened in fear and he edged closer to Tad until he bumped against his legs.

Tad settled a hand on the boy's shoulder. "Come on, Nate. Let's go clean up this mess." He smiled at Posey. "I'll keep an eye on him while you see to your errands."

"Thank you, Tad. I'll hurry," she said, taking a few rushed steps back in the direction she'd come.

He offered her a reassuring smile. "Take your time, Posey."

Tad led Nate back across the street to his shop. In the workroom, he showed Nate how to wipe the mud out of the saddlebags. When he was satisfied they were clean, he oiled the smooth leather then let it dry.

While they waited for the oil to soak into the leather, he let Nate play on the display saddles in the front of his shop.

"Is this one new, Uncle Tad?" Nate asked. He climbed on a saddle with a high cantle stained the color of black walnuts.

Tad smiled and ruffled the boy's golden brown hair. Sunlight had lightened streaks through the unruly strands. "It is a new saddle, Nate. What do you think of it?"

The boy rocked from side to side, adjusted his seat, and then scooted forward and back. He ran a small hand over the stamped leather along the skirt then grabbed a hold of the horn and gave it a few tugs. "It'll do."

Tad bit back a grin and tweaked the boy's nose. "I could say the same about you."

The little boy offered him a cheeky smile then bounced on the saddle. "You make the bestest saddles in the whole world!"

Tad chuckled. "I don't know about the whole world, but I do try to make good saddles, son. It's important to the cowboys who buy them to be able to trust the comfort and quality of my work."

"That's why everyone wants your saddles, Uncle Tad." The boy jumped down and ran over to a child-sized saddle at the end of the row. He often played on the butternut brown saddle, pretending it was on the back of a trusty steed.

Tad had tried numerous times to talk Posey into taking it for Nate, but she refused. If she gave in to the saddle, it meant a pony would soon follow, and she worried about Nate's safety.

Although Tad thought a pony would help teach Nate responsibility and give him a positive outlet for some of his excess energy, it wasn't his decision to make. No matter how much he might wish Posey and Nate were his, they weren't.

During the past four years, Tad had fought his attraction to his best friend's widow. He'd done everything he could think of to put her from his mind, but he couldn't. Not when he loved her more with every beat of his heart.

No matter what he felt for her, he knew Posey still loved John. And he couldn't blame her.

John Jacobs was the finest man Tad had ever known. He was certainly worthy of Posey's love, even years after his death. Mindful of the promise he'd made to his dying friend, Tad had vowed to watch over Posey and Nate, and that's exactly what he intended to do.

Watch over them. Protect them. Provide for them. Love them.

He'd done all he could to keep his love for Posey from shifting. Regardless, somewhere along the way, his feelings had changed from those of a friend to deep and abiding affection for a woman who wholly captivated him. But she'd never know. He certainly wouldn't be the one to tell her many a night he tossed and turned, envisioning the way sunlight glistened across her golden head or humor turned her eyes into deep molasses pools he could dive right into without a backward glance.

Nope. He'd go on pretending he felt nothing more than simple friendship for the woman and her son.

In truth, Nate was almost more than Posey could handle on her own. Bright, inquisitive, and fearless, the boy didn't seem hampered by the bounds that kept most children from hurtling head long into disaster. Combine that reckless spirit with an already mischievous, playful personality and it was no wonder Nate seemed to walk hand-in-hand with trouble.

The older the boy got, the more mischief he seemed to get into. Lately, Posey had seemed at her wits end to keep Nate from unintentionally hurting himself or someone else.

Posey would do well to fall in love and marry again. A woman with such kissable lips and a laugh that sounded like bells ringing straight from heaven shouldn't spend her days and nights alone. However, the thought of Posey marrying anyone made Tad's gut clench and the muscle in his jaw tick.

"What's wrong, Uncle Tad?" Nate asked, leaning against his thigh as he continued to sit on the small saddle.

"Nothing at all, son." Tad reached out, lifted the boy in his arms, and tickled the child's sides.

Nate squirmed and giggled as Tad carried him to the back room. He set the boy down then checked the saddlebags.

"Let's take these back to Mr. Lambery." Tad handed the bags to Nate.

The little boy nodded and marched to the front door. Rather than race across the street, Nate waited and took Tad's hand in his.

Together they walked to the saloon.

"Wait here, and do not move from that spot," Tad said, motioning for Nate to stay by the door. He stepped inside and located Joe. "We've got your saddlebags ready, Joe."

The man tipped back his hat and looked at Tad, expecting him to have the saddlebags. "Where are they?"

"Nate's holding them outside. I thought he should be the one to return them to you."

Joe narrowed his gaze. "Send him in, then."

Tad crossed his arms over his solid chest and frowned. "I'm not bringing that boy in here. If you don't want to come outside, we'll leave them where he found them in the first place. You're lucky someone didn't run off with them, just tossed over the hitching rail like that."

"I was keeping an eye on 'em," Joe whined.

Two of the men at the table snorted and a third spoke around the cigar dangling from one side of his mouth. "Be hard to do that since ya had one eye on your cards and the other on that bar maid over there." He tipped his head to a woman in a revealing dress filling a tray with glasses.

"Fine. I'll come get them," Joe said, tossing his cards on the table with a scowl. He stomped across the floor and gave the batwing doors such a hard shove as he strode through that the wood creaked while the hinges squealed in protest.

Nate stood exactly where Tad had left him, holding the saddlebags in his hands, although his attention appeared diverted by a piece of yellow string a few feet away on the worn boards of the boardwalk.

Joe grabbed the saddlebags from the boy. "Give me those." He opened the bags and stuck his hand inside each section, satisfied they were back to new condition. He tossed them over his shoulder then bent down and shook a finger in Nate's face. "I better not ever find you close to my things again or I'll forget you're a little kid and beat the stuffin' right out of you."

Nate gulped and scurried over to Tad, grasping his hand.

"There's no need to scare him half to death," Tad said, admonishing Joe.

"I'll scare him all the way there if he ever touches my things again. Make sure he tells his mother..."

"Tells me what?" Posey asked as she set a box in the back of her wagon and hurried over to where Tad and Nate stood outside the saloon.

Joe gave her a long perusal before he spoke. "If you don't mind my saying, Mrs. Jacobs, someone needs to take your boy in hand. What you need is a husband and a father for that boy."

Tad took a step away from Joe, pulling Nate with him as Posey marched closer to the man. He'd seen that particular determined look all too often and knew to stay out of her way when her temper was provoked.

All sweetness melted from her countenance like sugar in a cloudburst as she shook her finger in Joe's face. "Contrary to the opinion of the males in this town, I don't need a man, Mr. Lambery. I get along perfectly well on my own. As for my son, well, he's just lively and bright and curious, sometimes far too much for his own good. Regardless, I would greatly appreciate it if you refrain from commenting on the lack of a man in our lives. The very last reason I'd wed again is just to have a man to take my son in hand, as you put it. Good day."

She turned around and marched to her wagon, tugging Nate along beside her. Before she could reach down to swing him up to the seat, Tad stepped over and lifted the boy, tossing him in the air, eliciting a series of giggles.

"Do it again, Uncle Tad! Please?" Nate begged.

Tad tossed him again before setting the boy on the wagon seat. He then held out a hand to Posey and helped her climb up.

"I'm sorry Nate's naughtiness created more work for you," she said, sitting down and settling her skirts around her.

"Don't worry about it," Tad said, observing the pink dress with matching jacket Posey wore. He pondered if it was new. He didn't recall seeing her wear it before and he paid acute attention to how she appeared each time he saw her. The pale hue of her gown made her skin look like the porcelain dolls that lined a shelf at Miller's Mercantile. Flawless and smooth, with the slightest hint of a blush at her cheeks, he wondered if her skin would feel as good as it looked.

In spite of himself, Tad leaned forward slightly and took a deep breath, inhaling Posey's tantalizing floral fragrance. It made him think of the flowers that blossomed in his mother's conservatory back in Virginia. He couldn't think of the name of the flower, but the fragrance was one he knew well. In all the years he'd known Posey, her scent always made him think of a beautiful, delicate bloom.

The woman, though, had proven time and again that she could take care of herself. Even if he'd rather she allow him to help her more than he did, he admired her strength and determination to forge out a life for herself and Nate.

When he lifted his eyes from Posey's dress to her face, his gaze collided with hers. Perhaps wishing made him see things that weren't there. He thought he caught a flicker of longing in her expressive eyes. But that couldn't be.

Posey would never get over John. She'd just told Joe Lambery she had no intention of marrying again, so it was foolhardy to entertain even the slightest notion she might someday return his love.

Tad wasn't sure how he'd feel if she did, beyond the obvious emotions of elated and euphoric. Guilt ate at him every time he thought of John and the promise he'd made to his dying friend. He'd promised to take care of Posey and Nate, not take John's place.

Yet, as he stared into the intriguing depths of her eyes, Tad forgot about everything except how much he wanted to kiss her, to love her.

Posey leaned down toward him, as though she felt the magnetic pull to be together as much as he did.

What might have happened next would remain a mystery, though. Nate grabbed Posey's arm, jerking her and Tad back to reality.

"Mama, look!" The little boy stood and pointed to a cloud of dust rising on Main Street. The thundering sound of hooves preceded the sight of the sheriff and his two best friends racing pell-mell down the wide street.

"Looks like Tully, Maggie, and Thane are at it again," Posey mused, settling Nate back onto the seat next to her.

"So it would seem," Tad said, amused. "I don't think Tully Barrett has changed much since he became the sheriff."

Posey giggled as the riders raced back by, apparently vying for first place in a contest. "I'm glad. Tully keeps things from ever being dull, especially the way he, Thane, and Maggie are always up to something."

"I agree," Tad said, walking alongside the wagon as Posey released the brake and snapped the reins, sending the team into a slow walk toward Main Street.

"Will you join us for supper, Tad? I feel like I owe you something for helping clean up the mess Nate made of Mr. Lambery's saddlebags."

"You don't owe me anything, Posey, but I won't turn down an invitation to one of your fine meals." Tad smiled up at her. "Is there anything I can bring?"

"No. Just yourself and your appetite." She offered him an imploring grin. "Maybe your fiddle if you're in the mood to play after we eat."

He nodded in agreement. "I think that can be arranged."

"We'll see you at six," Posey said, then guided the wagon around the corner. Tad watched her wave at Maggie Dalton, who had won the competition against Sheriff Barrett and Thane Jordan.

He should have refused Posey's invitation and stayed away from the woman.

But when it came to her, Tad didn't possess a single lick of sense.

Chapter Three

Posey was glad she'd already completed most of her errands before trouble found her son in the form of mud pies.

If the little scamp wasn't so sweet and charming, she'd be completely exasperated with him. Loveable and smart, he made it nearly impossible to remain upset with him for long.

She'd known when he'd begged to wait by the wagon while she ran into the bank that he'd most likely get into some sort of mischief. Only gone a few moments, she had no idea how he filled Mr. Lambery's saddlebag with a mud pie so quickly. Nate had dutifully behaved while she stopped by the feed store for a load of supplies then went to the mercantile to pick up a few things she needed. The bank and post office were the last two stops on her list before heading for home.

Unfortunately, Nate got into trouble before she got as far as the post office.

If it wasn't for Tad's intercession, she wondered what Joe Lambery would have done to her son. The man was a shiftless, lazy schemer on a good day.

Threatening children didn't seem far-fetched at all considering his other transgressions.

No, Nate was lucky he chose to get in trouble right across the street from Tad's saddle shop. If she hadn't already felt so indebted to the kind-hearted man for everything he'd done to help her since John's death, she might have asked him to keep an eye on Nate.

If he happened to see her in town, he frequently took the boy back to his shop, allowing her the luxury of shopping in peace without worries of what Nate would get into.

For reasons she couldn't explain, Nate behaved well for Tad. Whatever the man said or suggested, her little boy did without question.

It might have left her baffled if she hadn't experienced a similar feeling anytime she was around the handsome man.

Tad was so different from John.

Posey had met her husband when she was fifteen. He'd hired on as a hand at her uncle's ranch. With both her parents gone and no other living relative, Posey had moved to Uncle Hiram's place when she was twelve. Her uncle did his best to raise her properly, but Posey had learned to ride, shoot, and work cattle right alongside the men. Then John, who seemed so worldly at the ripe old age of eighteen, rode onto the place and into her heart.

Despite her uncle's protests, she'd married John a week after she turned sixteen. A few months later, John decided they'd journey further west where he'd heard people were striking it rich in gold mines in Eastern Oregon.

After a tearful goodbye with her uncle, she left her Colorado home. On the way to Baker City, Oregon, she and John became friends with a young man named Theodore Palmer, who'd just left his home in Virginia.

Upon their arrival in the mining town, the two men set up a tent for Posey to live in then went to work in a mine. Before long, they started making money. The day John carried her across the threshold of the house he'd built for her a few miles from town, Posey thought all her dreams had come true.

And then Nate had arrived, making her feel even more blessed than she deserved. He'd been such a beautiful baby. She and John had spent hours studying each little toe and finger.

Life had been so perfect. They had good friends, a lovely home, and a bright future. Up until the day John died, Posey had lived in a constant state of harmony.

Dark, clawing pain had settled over her for a long time after John's death. With prayers, time, and Tad's dependable presence, she'd finally made her way out of her devastating grief and embraced life once again.

The depths of despair she felt upon losing her husband had convinced her that her heart had died that day, too.

Now, she knew better.

Slowly, sweetly, almost imperceptibly, she'd fallen in love with Tad Palmer. She couldn't even look back over the past four years and pinpoint the moment she'd realized she loved Tad.

He'd gone from being her husband's best friend and her rock during her overwhelming grief to being her best friend, champion, protector, and encourager. Tad was one of her many reasons to smile, even if he didn't realize it.

For the most part, Tad was quiet and reserved. Yet, he'd become someone the town depended on. She knew Sheriff Barrett often called on Tad when he was in need of an extra deputy. Tad could be found helping several ranchers in the area, like Thane Jordan, or providing a hand wherever it was needed. She'd even seen him assisting the new lumberyard owner one evening as the man burnt his brand onto stacks of fragrant pine boards.

Tad was also generous. He contributed to the widow and orphan funds, anonymously purchased supplies for those in need, and did little things for people without them ever knowing who was their benefactor.

If Posey hadn't been watching Tad so closely, she would never have known half of the charitable things he'd done.

But watching him was one of the things that brought her great pleasure.

Heat suffused her face as she brought to mind a vision of Tad's broad shoulders and muscled form. She'd memorized everything about him from the thatch of thick, dark hair on his head to the scruffy beard on his face that didn't quite hide the dimple in his all-too-attractive chin. Square jawed, blue eyed, and with lips that appeared to have been sculpted by an artist, it was a wonder the man remained unwed.

Thoughts of him marrying anyone made her stomach clench in pain. More than anything, she wanted Tad to be happy, but the thought of his happiness coming from another woman left her agitated and unsettled.

So badly, she wanted to be the one he loved.

But even after all this time, he seemed completely indifferent to her, to her feelings for him.

Afraid if she finally worked up the courage to tell him the truth he'd rebuff her, she'd remained silent, admiring him, longing for him without letting on how she really felt.

Today, though, as he stared up at her, she thought she'd seen something flicker in his eyes. Something that gave her hope that perhaps not all was yet lost.

If it hadn't been for Nate pointing out the sheriff racing like a wild hooligan through town with his friends, she wondered if Tad might have actually kissed her.

"Don't be ridiculous, Posey Jo Jacobs," she admonished herself.

"What'd you say, Mama?" Nate asked, leaning against her side.

"Nothing, baby." Posey bent over and placed a kiss on his forehead. "What do you think we should make for supper tonight?"

"Meat! Tad likes meat and potatoes." Nate grinned up at her. "And pie!"

"Pie and meat, hmm?" Posey smiled. "You sound like your papa. He always liked meat and pie, too."

"My papa was Uncle Tad's bestest friend, huh?" Nate looked to her for confirmation of the fact he already knew.

"That's right, baby. Uncle Tad was your daddy's best friend. They worked side by side for a long time in a mine and then Uncle Tad opened his saddle shop."

"Uncle Tad said I look like Papa. Do I, Mama? Do I look like him?" The hopeful look on her son's face tugged at Posey's heart.

She shifted the reins to one hand so she could cup his chin with her other as she looked him square in the face. "You look exactly like your daddy. Your hair is a little lighter than his was, but you have his eyes and nose, his smile and strong chin. You even have the same cowlick in your hair right here." She ran her fingers through a spot near Nate's temple where his hair always looked unkempt despite her best efforts to tame it. "I think you'll grow up to be a fine, wonderful, handsome man just like your papa."

Nate remained silent for a few moments as Posey returned to holding the reins with both hands. She guided the team off the road onto their lane.

"Mama?" Nate gave her another questioning glance.

"What is it, sweetheart?" Posey glanced at him before returning her attention to stopping the wagon then directing the horses to back it into the open shed where she kept it out of the weather.

"Would it be bad if I want to grow up to be like Uncle Tad? He's smart and funny, and he's awful nice to me."

Posey smiled. "It would be a grand thing to want to grow up like him, Nate. I can't think of a man I know that's any better than your Uncle Tad."

"Oh, good!" Nate jumped down from the wagon the moment it stopped and took off running. He opened the gate to a pen on the side of the barn and giggled as a goat rushed out and rubbed against him. "Hi, Agnes. Did you miss me?"

The goat bleated in response and trotted after him as the boy raced back to the wagon to help Posey unload it. She handed Nate bags and baskets he could carry while she unloaded the heavier items.

No doubt, Tad would willingly unload everything for her when he came for supper if she asked him to do it, but she liked to be self-sufficient. As she struggled to drag a heavy sack of grain to the barn, she began to second think her decision to ask Tad for help.

She took a deep breath and hefted the bag, barely scooting it inside the barn before her strength gave out.

"Whew! I think that's enough of that for right now," she said, dabbing at the moisture gathering along her hairline with a handkerchief she pulled from her pocket.

Nate giggled and ran across the yard with the goat trailing along beside him like an obedient dog.

Posey shook her head, gathered the box of foodstuffs she'd purchased at the mercantile and headed into the house to prepare dinner. The rest of the sacks in the wagon could wait until tomorrow.

Inside her kitchen, Posey stoked the stove and put away her purchases then started to go change. In a moment of vanity, she decided to leave on the new pink dress that made her feel feminine and attractive. Vainly, she'd hoped Tad had noticed she wore a new gown, but he hadn't given any indication. Then again, he'd never commented on her appearance. Most likely, he looked at her as he would his sister.

Discouraged, but determined to do her best to catch his eye, Posey slipped on her fullest apron and started meal preparations. As soon as she slipped a pie in the oven to bake, she began heating a curling iron.

While it heated, she peeled potatoes then set them to boil. Finished with the task, she took down her hair, combed it, and pinned it up again. She added a few well-placed curls around her face and left three long tendrils hanging down her back along the right side of her neck.

Nate ran inside just as she completed the hairstyle. The goat bleated and followed him into the kitchen.

"Not in the house, Nathaniel John Jacobs! Agnes has to stay outside." Posey waggled her finger at the door.

"Aw, Mama, Agnes just wants to have dinner with us. Why can't she stay?"

Nate gave her such an imploring look, Posey wanted to give in. Instead, she scowled when the goat sidled toward the linen cloth covering the table.

"Outside, this instant, young man, before she eats my tablecloth and your supper. Now scoot!"

Nate scuffed his toes all the way to the door, but the goat obediently followed him outside.

Posey sliced thick pieces of smoky ham and put it on to fry, then opened a can of corn she'd preserved from her garden last fall and set it to heat. She topped slices of bread with butter then sprinkled them with cheese she'd shredded and a few dried herbs. As soon as Tad arrived, she'd pop them into the oven to toast.

After removing the pie from the oven, she hurried to set the table. She was just about to call Nate inside to wash up when she noticed Tad riding up to the house on his saddle horse.

Admiration filled her as he rode up to her front gate with the sun at his back. He cut such a striking figure, all she could do was stare for the length of several heartbeats. Tad appeared strong enough to take on any challenge life might throw his way. She wondered, then, why it was he seemed so hesitant to pursue a relationship with her.

Maybe he just didn't find her attractive. Perhaps he didn't experience those tingling feelings throughout his whole body each time they accidentally touched as she did. The thought that her fascination with the man was entirely one-sided made her nervous and unsettled.

Nevertheless, for one evening she vowed to be bold and brave. She would act as though she was a carefree, charming young woman, not a widow with a puckish son, a loony goat, and a small farm that needed more work than she could give it.

Through the open window, she heard the creak of leather as Tad swung out of the saddle and listened as he greeted her son and his beloved pet.

"Hey, Nate. What are you and Agnes doing?" She peeked out the window and saw Tad hunker down so he was on eye level with the boy. He reached out a hand and brushed it over Agnes' neck, giving her a good scratch.

"Mama kicked us out of the house. She said Agnes couldn't stay for dinner." Nate pouted.

"You don't say." Tad's voice held a hint of humor as he stood and looped the reins around a post near the gate. "I reckon we better make sure Agnes has some dinner out here, then."

"Yep," Nate said, taking Tad's hand and tugging him toward the barn. "I'll show you her feed."

Posey raced into her bedroom and dabbed on a bit of perfume then checked her image in the dresser mirror. She pinched her cheeks, to add a bit of color, arranged a few curls around her face, and rushed back to the kitchen.

By the time Tad and Nate stamped their feet at the back door, the meal was ready and she was just setting the last bowl of food on the table.

"Evening, Posey," Tad said, holding his hat in his hands as he stepped inside.

"Evening, Tad. Wash up and take a seat. Supper's getting cold." She grabbed Nate's hands in hers and directed him over to the sink. Tad pumped water while she helped her son wash his hands, then Nate insisted on pumping the handle while Tad washed.

Together, the two of them approached the table where she stood waiting.

Tad pulled out her chair and waited for her to be seated before he scooted in Nate's chair then took the seat across from the boy. The chair at the head of the table remained empty — a stark reminder of the loss they all suffered when John died.

Posey wouldn't have cared if Tad had wanted to sit in John's chair, but he'd never once, in all the meals he'd eaten with them, shown any inclination to take that seat.

"Tad, would you ask the blessing on our meal?" Posey asked. She bowed her head as Tad's rich voice filled the kitchen with words of gratitude.

"Amen!" Nate said at the end of the prayer. He plopped his napkin on his lap then looked over the meal before him. "I'm hungry, Mama!"

"Then let's get you fed, son." Posey smiled as she dished food onto Nate's plate, cut his meat, and moved his glass of milk away from the edge of the table before the boy could spill it.

"This looks delicious, Posey. Do you need more meat?" Tad asked as he helped himself to a large slice of ham.

"No. I still have a few hams, some bacon, and one beef roast left from the meat you so generously brought the last time you decided to restock my supplies." She gave him a narrowed glare. "You do realize that isn't necessary, don't you? I can provide for Nate and myself."

"I know," Tad said, nodding in agreement. He pointed his fork at the platter of ham. "But I have to do something to repay you for all the groceries I eat when you invite me over."

"Tad, you do far more work around here than you could ever eat in the meals we share with you. No matter what you say or think, I know better."

He grinned and took a bite of the cheesy bread. "I don't know what it is about this bread, but it is so good."

Posey placed another slice on his plate. "It's just cheese, butter, a few dried herbs, and bread. You could make it at your place anytime you wanted."

"I've tried. It doesn't taste the same as when you do it, so I guess I'll have to go on eating it here and you'll have to keep on accepting the supplies I bring in trade."

Exasperated, she shook her head. "There's no arguing with you, is there, Tad Palmer?"

"Nope." He gave her a rakish wink that made her heart skitter in her chest before he turned to Nate. "Have you taught Agnes any new tricks this week, Nate?"

The boy shook his head. "No. I tried to teached her to bark like a doggie, but she just does this..." Nate made a series of loud goat-like sounds before Posey rolled her eyes at Tad.

"We get the idea, son," she said, scooting his milk away from the edge of the table again. While Nate took a bite of mashed potatoes covered in gravy, she turned to Tad. "Did you finally receive a letter from your sister? I know the last time we talked about Gloria you were hoping to hear from her soon."

Tad smiled and wiped his mouth on his napkin. "I did receive a letter from her just today. She and Colin are in Europe on tour and having a wonderful time. I still can't believe my little sister is such an accomplished pianist, as is her husband."

"I think it's wonderful they share so much in common. From what you've said, she and Mr. McDougal seem well-suited to one another." Posey gave him a long look. "You were worried for a while she might marry that dreadful Mr. Welbourne. I'm glad she realized that would never work and allowed herself to open her heart to Mr. McDougal."

"Yes, well, Mother was none too pleased about it, but Father supported Gloria's choice wholeheartedly."

Posey had often wondered about Tad's family and his past. He spoke with open affection about his only sibling. Gloria was seven years younger and the apple of her big brother's eye. She knew it had been hard on Tad to leave Gloria behind when he left his family home at such a young age. From tidbits he'd shared, she knew Tad kept in touch with Gloria through letters. He'd even gone to her wedding the previous summer, travelling back to Virginia to the place of his birth.

Yet, when she asked about his parents, he generally kept his answers vague and brief. Something, or someone, in his past had hurt him. Deeply. Regardless of his hesitance to share details about his mother and father, he spoke fondly about the ranch his father owned in Kansas and the summers he spent there as a boy, learning how to work leather and make saddles from an old cowboy named Butch.

Since it wasn't her place to pry into his past, Posey had never pressed Tad for more details about his family. She hoped he'd someday tell her his whole story, but even if he didn't, she could tell he loved his sister. She'd even noticed he held a great deal of admiration for his new brother-in-law.

Gloria had met Colin McDougal through her music, although Tad hadn't elaborated much more than that. Posey knew Gloria had earned a scholarship to play at the prestigious Marlowe Conservatory of Music. Mr. McDougal worked at the school.

From things Tad had mentioned, Posey arrived at the conclusion the Palmer family had a little money to spare, especially since the few photos she'd seen of the family made them appear quite well-to-do.

Tad shared much in common with his father, from his handsome appearance to his bearing. Gloria was beautiful, with a crown of rich, luxurious hair. Tad had told her it was auburn and that his sister's eyes were green. She resembled her mother, although Emmeline Palmer lacked the easy warmth so evident in Gloria and Tad.

Mindful of Tad's feelings on the subject of his parents, she guided the conversation back to Gloria's music.

Tad played the fiddle well, although he kept the fact to himself. He'd told Posey if everyone found out he could play, he'd end up having to join the musicians at every community dance instead of sweeping her across the floor.

Posey rather liked the notion of being in Tad's arms, even for the short time a dance or two lasted.

Thinking about those strong, solid arms wrapped around her, she gazed at him, lost in her daydreams and missed his question.

"Is that okay with you?" he asked, awaiting her response.

"I'm sorry, Tad. I must have been woolgathering." A flush warmed her cheeks to have been caught with her thoughts elsewhere. At least Tad didn't know they lingered on how attractive she found him, especially with that slight growth of stubble on his face. It only served to accent the enticing shape of his lips and the tempting dimple in his chin. Posey

43

had dreamed so many times of kissing that spot then working her way up to his tempting mouth.

Mortified by her wayward thoughts, she straightened in her chair while Tad smirked at her. "Just what, exactly, are you thinking?"

"Never mind," she said, handing him the bowl of corn just to have something to do.

Tad shook his head as he took the bowl from her and added a scoop of corn to his plate. "You were thinking something that made you look as guilty as all get out, Posey Jo. You better fess up."

A warm, molten feeling began in the pit of her stomach. It worked its way out to every extremity at his use of the name only he called her. Even John had never called her Posey Jo.

Something about the way Tad said it, the way his voice seemed to caress it, always left her languid and delighted. That name and the way it rolled off his tongue gave her hope that he might care for her more than she knew.

"I'm not confessing anything. Now, please repeat your question." Posey gave him an imperial look that drew out a broad smile.

Tad watched her face for a moment, making her want to squirm under his intent perusal. She wondered what he saw, what he thought when he looked at her that way.

Finally, he spoke. "I asked if you minded joining Tully, Maggie, and Thane after church Sunday. Maggie is making Easter dinner at Tully's. Her apartment is too small to hold very many people and Thane lives too far out of town, not that his cabin could hold many anyway. Tully has the biggest place and it's close to town. They invited us to join them, but I wanted to make sure you didn't have other plans."

Posey liked that Tad thought in terms of them being an "us" and he wanted to pay heed to her preferences. "That sounds wonderful, Tad. I'll get in touch with Maggie. I was planning on fixing a big meal anyway, so perhaps Maggie would like to hold it here. I'm sure my kitchen is better suited to preparing a big meal than the sheriff's."

Tad grinned. "Most likely. I'm not sure Tully knows one end of a frying pan from the other."

Posey laughed and gave Tad a pointed glare. "And you do? Last time I checked, you weren't overly proficient in the kitchen."

"Well, that's because you insist on keeping me well fed most of the time."

"That's not true. You only eat with us once or twice a week. Back when we first moved here, you joined John and me every day for meals."

"That's because I lived in the tent next to yours and we pooled our funds to buy food." Tad's smile faded. "Do you ever miss those days, Posey?"

Somber, she nodded. "As crazy as it sounds, I do. But life has become sweet again and I wouldn't trade time spent with you two for anything." She ruffled a hand through Nate's disheveled hair, drawing a smile from the boy as he ate the last bite of his bread.

"I'm done, Mama. May I please be excused?"

At her nod, he jumped off his chair and hurried out the door.

"Stay in the yard!" she called after him before he slammed the door behind him.

Out the window, Posey saw Nate running back and forth through the grass with Agnes. The farm dog had come out of hiding and lounged in the shade of a tree, watching the boy and goat.

"I've never seen anything like that goat out there," Tad mused, pointing to the goat as it leaped over the fence. Nate hurried to open the gate and coax her back into the yard.

"Agnes is one of a kind." Posey stood and started clearing the table. She turned from setting dishes in the sink to find Tad standing close behind her, holding dirty plates.

Caught off guard by his proximity, she took a deep breath, inhaling his masculine scent blended with a whiff of leather. Tad always smelled of leather. Posey drew another deep breath, relishing the aroma.

She glanced up and saw something heated flicker in his blue eyes. Convinced she imagined the emotion in his expression, she took the plates from him and set them in the sink. When she turned back around, he'd moved away, picking up more of the dishes.

Later, after they'd enjoyed slices of warm peach pie made from her precious stash of canned peaches, Tad leaned back in his chair and rubbed a hand over his flat belly.

"See, if I ate like this every night, I'd be as big around as a wash tub and only slightly less spry."

Posey laughed. "I highly doubt that, Tad Palmer. You work too hard to put on any extra weight."

"Still, it's best I not be tempted by your good cooking too often." His heated look made her heart accelerate again. "You offer any number of temptations I find hard to resist."

Uncertain if Tad referred to her cooking or something else, Posey ignored the excited fluttering in her stomach and rose to her feet. "Want to see my latest project?"

"Of course," Tad said, following her down the hall to a bedroom she'd converted into her workroom.

As a widow with a baby, Posey turned her talent for quilting into a business. The mercantile and Tad both carried the quilts she made. She also created special order quilts. Since the house John had built for her had three bedrooms, she'd converted the extra bedroom into a place to do her quilting. Tad had built quilt frames that were lightweight and easy for her to set up by herself. He'd also insisted she be the first to use one of the new sewing machines he began carrying in his shop.

Posey could sew a simple quilt top in a day with the sewing machine and, working steadily, could have a quilt ready to sell in a week.

Tad had suggested she sell The Limitless Mine after John's death and she hadn't argued. He'd found a buyer and made sure she got a fair price for it. The funds from the mine sale had gone a long way in providing for her and Nate, but she knew she'd eventually need a source of income. So she took her love of stitching and creating quilts and turned it into a profitable enterprise.

One Tad had whole-heartedly supported.

Posey stepped into the room and motioned to a dark blue and white quilt she had in the frame. Nearly half of it bore beautiful stitching, the result of tedious quilting.

Tad wiped his hand along the side of his trousers before reaching out to touch intricate stitches she worked into a white square of fabric surrounded by blue squares with a white flower pattern sewn into the center.

"I like this one, Posey. What's it called?" he asked, bending closer to study her fine work.

"Wandering Foot." She smiled as she picked up a small pair of scissors and snipped a loose thread.

Tad laughed. "And who is this one for?"

"Mrs. Hilldebrand ordered it as a going away gift for the Lamond family. They're leaving in two weeks to move to Oregon City."

He chuckled. "Well, it's a fitting title for it, then. Isn't this about the third time the Lamonds have moved back here and left again?"

"Yes, I believe it is. I feel sorry for Mrs. Lamond and the children. It must be so hard to move every year or so." Posey glanced out the window and watched Nate playing with Agnes, the dog, and two fuzzy gray kittens. "I like staying in one place. Staying here."

Tad nodded in agreement. "When we first moved here, I wasn't sure Baker City would ever feel like home, but it certainly does now. I wouldn't want to live elsewhere."

She cocked her head and offered him a saucy smile. "We wouldn't let you leave, even if you wanted to. Nate and I would miss you far too much."

"We'll, I'm glad to hear that," Tad said. He took something from his pocket and handed it to her.

She accepted the small parcel, wrapped in a scrap of blue cloth and tied with a bit of string. "What's this?" Her eyes lifted to his in question.

"Just something I made." Tad stepped back and shrugged, shoving his hands in his pockets.

With him eyeing her expectantly, Posey untied the string then turned back the fabric, revealing a piece of leather shaped like the finger of a glove.

Uncertain, she looked to Tad.

He grinned and picked up the leather sleeve, sliding it over the middle finger on her right hand. The soft leather molded to her finger. "It's a quilting thimble. I thought you might like it, rather than a traditional hard thimble."

"Oh, it's lovely, Tad." Posey sat in the chair next to the quilt and picked up the needle she'd poked into the fabric to mark her place. She quickly quilted several stitches then smiled up at him. "It's wonderful, Tad! I love it!" Without giving a thought to her actions, she jumped to her feet and offered him an exuberant hug. "Thank you!"

Although he hesitated at first, eventually his arms wrapped around her and he returned her hug. His chuckles vibrated through her as she stood with her cheek pressed against his chest. "If I'd known I'd get a reaction like this out of you, I would have made that silly thing a long time ago."

Posey grinned. "Just imagine what might happen if you make me another."

He made a sound deep in his throat that could have been a growl before he expelled a long sigh and stepped away from her.

Posey felt bereft without his arms around her, but she had no right to ask him to hold her again.

She certainly had no right to beg him to love her, although it was on the tip of her tongue to say the words.

Before the moment grew serious, she removed the thimble and left it on the quilt, leading the way back to the kitchen. She poured a cup of coffee and handed it to him then leaned against the counter.

"Do I get my concert tonight?" she asked.

"What concert might that be?" Tad feigned ignorance.

"You playing the fiddle. That concert." She waggled her finger toward the window. "I can see your fiddle case on the saddle. Why don't we take our coffee outside and you can play on the porch?"

Tad followed her outside and handed her his cup. "I didn't know Agnes and the other critters needed musical inspiration."

"Of course, they do." Posey set their cups on a table between two rocking chairs and took a seat.

Nate ran over and climbed up on her lap. The dog and kittens joined them on the porch. Agnes jumped up and walked across the top of the porch railing while Tad took the fiddle out of the case and tuned the strings.

As he launched into a lively tune, Posey leaned back and watched his every move. She loved to see his fingers dance across the strings, his broad shoulders bowed slightly forward as he played.

With his sister's talent at the piano, she assumed Tad's musical abilities had to be something he inherited, although he claimed neither his mother nor father seemed particularly musical. While he played just for fun, Gloria's music was something he referred to as a God-given gift.

Nate leaned back against her and clapped his little hands as Tad segued into another fast song.

Throughout his concert, she studied him, elated he shared something so special with them, yet saddened that he felt the need to hide his talent from others.

Considering how stubborn he was, about everything from playing the fiddle in front of others to paying what he saw as his dues, she wondered how hard she'd have to work to change his mind.

Posey held back a sigh. How could she convince the thickheaded man she was irrevocably in love with him?

SHANNA HATFIELD

Chapter Four

Tad clenched his jaw as Sheriff Tully Barrett leaned close to Posey and said something that made her smile. The man had been particularly attentive to her throughout the meal, drawing Tad's scrutiny and irritation.

He'd never noticed the sheriff expressing any interest in Posey before, so he wondered why the friendly, good-looking man of the law suddenly seemed intent on hovering around her.

Right after the church service, Tad had driven Posey and Nate back to their little farm where she'd arranged with Maggie Dalton to host Easter dinner.

Maggie had agreed Posey's kitchen would be far easier to use than Tully's and had no problem in moving their gathering from his place.

Tad admired the close friendship shared by Tully, Maggie, and Thane Jordan. They'd been friends since they all arrived in Baker City, close to the time he had arrived with Posey and John. Tully and Thane had worked with Maggie's husband in a mine until Daniel Dalton was killed.

After his death, the two friends kept watch over Maggie, much as Tad had kept an eye on Posey.

While Tad had fallen head over heels in love with Posey, neither Tully or Thane appeared enamored with Maggie. In fact, they acted like siblings, constantly teasing and arguing with each other.

If Tad hadn't already been so blinded with love for Posey, he might have given Maggie a second glance. The woman was beautiful with her dark hair and eyes, vibrant personality, and no-nonsense approach to life. Fun and witty, Maggie was also a fine horsewoman not to mention a talented seamstress. She ran her own dressmaking shop just around the corner and down the street from his business.

Then again, he had no intention to wed. If things had been different, if Posey had been open to accepting his love, he might have considering breaking the promise he made himself to remain single. Since she clearly would never love anyone but John, Tad could love her from afar and maintain his plans to remain unattached.

A conniving girl and his mother had made certain he was indefinitely soured on marriage and relationships. Arabella had been so beautiful. The first time Tad had set eyes on her when he was seventeen he'd been smitten with her. She used that to her advantage, worming her way into his affections and scheming with his mother to become his bride. Enamored with the girl, Tad would have given her the world on a silver platter. Then he'd found her ardently kissing one of his so-called friends. When he confronted them both, Arabella confessed she didn't truly care for him and had only gone along with his mother's plans to unite their families and further her wealthy ambitions.

Heartbroken and devastated, Tad had packed his things and left. The only money he took with him was what he'd earned himself from work he'd done on the Kansas ranch. He'd thought about going there to live, but decided he needed to get farther away from his parents and their connections, so he made his way to Oregon.

In the process, he'd met John and Posey Jacobs. And for that, he was forever grateful.

Tad pulled his thoughts back to those gathered at Posey's home to celebrate Easter, studying the guests. Even if he was interested in Maggie, and he most definitely wasn't, it appeared the woman's indifference to the lumberyard owner didn't thwart Ian McGregor's interest in her.

Posey and Maggie were the only women at the gathering of friends, which wasn't unusual since the number of men in the area far outnumbered women.

Ian, Tully, one of his deputies, Thane, and a few of Thane's ranch hands who attended the church service were gathered at Posey's place. Tad noticed all the men offered friendly attention to both widows, although Tully appeared to be the only one paying particular interest to Posey.

When the sheriff bent down and whispered something in Posey's ear, Tad sprang out of his seat. He marched across the yard to where the two of them stood near a table holding refreshments.

"Hey, Sheriff, have you had any leads on the men who stole Mr. Mason's barber's pole?" Tad asked, thumping his hand on Tully's back and drawing the man's attention away from Posey.

Tully turned his head and gave Tad a puzzled look before responding. "No. I haven't."

"It's ridiculous that someone would steal Mr. Mason's barber's pole. What on earth would anyone want with it?" Posey asked, looking from Tully to Tad. Tension pulsed between the two men, although the cause of it remained a mystery.

Clearly uncomfortable, Posey glanced over at the food table and noticed Nate about to make himself sick by eating too many sweet treats. "Excuse me, gentlemen," she said, rushing over to her son.

Tully gave Tad one more glance and then tipped his head to him. "Palmer."

"Sheriff." Tad's voice sounded tight and strained as he spoke. It was all he could do to keep from punching Tully in the nose when the man sauntered over to where Posey made Nate choose from the array of desserts on his plate.

The sheriff hunkered down and said something to the little boy that made him smile broadly. Nate grabbed two cookies, shoved the rest of the sweets on his plate at his mother, and sauntered off with Tully.

Annoyed with the man for charming Posey and Nate, Tad tried to tamp down his jealousy. He had no right to be upset, no reason to be angry.

Posey was free to choose any man she wanted to court. Tully Barrett was an honorable, upright, good person who'd make a solid husband and a kind father. But the very notion of anyone other than him wooing

Posey and filling a fatherly role with Nate made Tad see red.

If a possibility existed to tuck Nate in of an evening and hold Posey all through the night, Tad wanted the job.

On the verge of losing his temper, he strode over to where Posey stared down at the plate Nate had filled with slices of pie and cake and took if from her hands. He grabbed a fork and viciously jabbed a bite, holding it out to her.

Surprise flickered across her face as she accepted a forkful of lemon meringue pie from him. Tad cut off a huge bite and stuffed it in his mouth. Despite his irritation, the burst of citrus flavor and sweetness filled his mouth and he glanced down at the pie in appreciation. "Did you make this?" he asked after he chewed and swallowed.

Posey nodded. "Yes. Maggie made the canned cherry pie and the layer cake. I made the lemon meringue pie and chocolate pie."

"It's really good, Posey," Tad said, cutting another small bite and holding it out to her.

She took it and gave him a strange look he chose to ignore.

After he finished the lemon pie, he moved on to the piece of cake on the plate. He held a bite out to Posey, but she refused.

He shrugged and ate it, barely tasting the rich, buttery frosting as he watched Posey's gaze travel to where Tully showed Nate how to load his slingshot with rocks.

No doubt, they all would regret the boy learning how to shoot it, but it kept him occupied, at least momentarily. Nate had been quite distraught to discover Agnes and Spot, the dog, were banned from the yard during their outdoor Easter feast. He'd moped around throughout the meal, despite Tad and Posey's efforts to engage him. Glad to see him enthusiastic about something, Tad just wished it had been him to put a smile on the child's face.

Thane joined Tully in showing Nate how to shoot rocks at an old tin can target they set up a few feet away.

"I envision a future of broken windows," Posey said, drawing Tad's attention back to her.

He grinned and nodded his head. "Perhaps you can stress the importance of never shooting it at the house, the animals, or you."

Posey laughed. The sound made his heart flop around in his chest like a floundered fish.

"If you wouldn't mind giving him that instruction, I'd appreciate it. Nate hangs on your every word." She poured a cup of punch while Tad finished eating the plate full of sweets.

He didn't know what possessed him to take it from her, to force her to share a few tastes with him. Thoughts of feeding her bites of dessert drew his gaze to her pink mouth. Not for the first time he wondered at the flavor of her kisses. Would they be sweet and light, or dark and rich? Just contemplating the possibilities made his mouth go so dry, he choked on the bite of cake he attempted to swallow.

Concerned, Posey handed him the cup of punch in her hands. He gulped it down and took a staggering step forward when Tully whopped him on the back with more force than was necessary.

"You okay, Palmer?" Tully asked, giving him another thump for good measure.

"I will be if you don't loosen something vital," Tad said, glaring over his shoulder at the sheriff.

Tully stood a little taller than Tad, his shoulders a little broader, but they would have been well matched if they ever came to blows.

Stricken by the direction of his thoughts, Tad couldn't believe he was actually considering pummeling his friend simply because he'd paid attention to Posey.

Any single man with eyes in his head would have been hard pressed not to notice how stunning she looked in a dress the color of ripening peaches. That particular shade brought out golden flecks in her warm brown eyes. The sunshine gliding across her hair made it glisten like spun gold.

Posey Jacobs was a very beautiful, desirable woman. One Tad could not get out of his system no matter how hard he tried.

Truth to tell, he didn't really want to.

But every time he thought about confessing his feelings to her, he'd think about John, about the promise he made to his friend. He owed it to John to watch over Posey. To protect her, to shelter her, to make sure she and Nate were well provided for. He couldn't help it if he'd fallen in love with her in the process.

Who could blame him for falling for the woman with her appealing curves, tender heart, and ability to make his day brighter just by gifting him with a smile.

Tad swallowed a groan of misery and forked a hand through his hair in frustration.

"Are you sure you're well, Tad?" Posey asked, placing a delicate hand on his arm.

"I'm fine. Just fine," he said, moving away from her. He needed a few minutes to gather his composure and calm his temper before he got himself into trouble.

He strode out of the yard and disappeared around the corner of the barn where he could have a few moments of quiet. He leaned back against the side of the barn and closed his eyes, letting the sunshine warm his face and the silence settle the turbulent state of his heart.

"Uncle Tad?" Nate asked, tugging on his pant leg.

"What is it, Nater?" Tad asked, using his nickname for the boy as he slid down the wall until he was on eye level with the boy.

"Are you sad, Uncle Tad?" Nate leaned against him. His eyes, so like his mother's, filled with worry.

"No, son, I'm just fine. After all, it's Easter, a day to rejoice and be grateful. Right?"

"That's what Pastor Eagan said, and he wouldn't lie," Nate said, resting against Tad when the man opened his arms to him.

The little boy leaned into his chest and sighed.

Tad lifted Nate in his arms and stood. "What's wrong, Nater?"

"Nothin', Uncle Tad. My eyeballs are sleepy."

Tad hid a smile. "They do that sometimes, don't they? Why don't you shut them and give them a little rest? It's just us men here. It's okay if you let them sleep a little bit."

"Okay, Uncle Tad," Nate whispered as he nestled his little face against Tad's neck.

Tad breathed in the combined scents of sunshine, goat, dog, and a whiff of lemon from the piece of pie the boy had eaten.

He took another whiff and grinned, thinking the only thing that smelled better than the little boy in his arms was the woman he longed to hold.

Tad leaned back against the barn and held Nate as he slept. The boy was worn out from a busy day and Tad didn't mind a few minutes just to hold the child. In the past four years, he'd held Nate plenty. He'd chased away tears, doctored cuts, wiped his nose, helped him learn to walk and talk.

Nate might not be his son by blood, but the boy was the child of his heart. Tad couldn't have loved him any more if he'd belonged to him from birth.

Posey and Nate were his two great loves and the thing that threatened to rip his heart right out of his chest was the thought that neither one of them would ever belong to him.

Chapter Five

Posey leaned on the handle of the shovel she held in her hands and took a moment to catch her breath. She'd spent the last hour cleaning out the milk cow's stall in the barn then restoring order in the chicken coop.

While she worked, she kept an eye on Nate. He'd been playing in the side yard with Agnes and Spot, but everything had grown strangely quiet. Nate was nowhere in sight which usually meant trouble was in the making.

Concerned by the type of mischief the little imp had most likely gotten into, she quickly finished working in the chicken coop, set aside the shovel, and went in search of her son. She'd told him to stay in the yard, and he usually minded. She wondered if he'd perhaps moved to the far side or back of the yard, beyond her view.

Hurried steps took her through the gate in the fence surrounding the yard. A fence Tad had insisted on building when Nate had started walking. Although she protested at him providing the materials and labor when he did it, she'd been grateful so many times for the safety the fence had offered for her son while she worked.

As she strolled through the yard she noticed the two kittens playing with a bit of yarn on the steps and the dog lounging nearby.

"Where's Nate, Spot? Huh, boy?" She spoke to the dog as she walked past him.

The dog lifted his head and cocked one ear then whined, as if to say, "he's fine." Reassured if Nate were in danger the dog would be right beside him, she continued around the front of the house.

Although she expected to discover Nate doing something he shouldn't, she wasn't quite prepared for the sight that greeted her when she located her son in the back yard.

"What on earth are you doing to poor Agnes, baby?" Posey stifled a giggle as she took in the vision of Agnes in a washtub full of soap bubbles and a drenched Nate scrubbing the goat's head.

"Giving her a bath. She smells funny." Nate wrinkled his nose as he rubbed Posey's perfumed French soap over the goat's head.

To her credit, Agnes seemed to enjoy the delicate fragrance of the soap and the attention lavished on her from the boy. The goat smiled in bliss as she closed her eyes and basked in the experience.

"Oh, Nate," Posey said, sinking down on her knees beside the washtub. She hated to see the expensive soap wasted, but the goat certainly appeared to be enjoying it. Nate looked almost as happy as Agnes did and Posey couldn't bring herself to chastise him. Despite her lofty position as Nate's favorite pet, Agnes was still a goat and probably had stunk.

"Am I in trouble, Mama?" Nate asked. His hands stilled in their scrubbing as he looked at her with big, earnest eyes.

"No, baby. But next time please use the soap from the kitchen, not Mama's bath soap." Posey lathered her hands and scratched along Agnes' back. If the goat could have purred, Posey thought she might have at that point.

Nate glanced down at the soap, then at his mother. "I'm sorry, Mama. I just wanted Agnes to smell pretty like you."

Touched by her son's sweet words and unintentional flattery, Posey nodded. "I know, sweetheart. Just ask next time before you use something of mine, please."

"Okay, Mama." Nate returned to scrubbing soap over the goat. Posey helped him rinse Agnes then went inside to make sandwiches for lunch. Since the day was so lovely and warm, she served the meal outside on the porch.

Agnes pranced around the yard, showing off her sparkling clean state to the dog and kittens.

"I think that goat is preening," Posey muttered, amused by Agnes.

"What's that mean, Mama?" Nate asked, holding his sandwich with both hands.

"Preening?"

Nate nodded and took a bite of the ham and bread.

"Well, it means to take pride in something. In the case of Agnes, she seems quite proud to be clean."

"It's good to be clean and smell nice, isn't it?"

Posey smiled. "It is, indeed, son. Perhaps you can remember that the next time I tell you it's time for a bath."

Nate grinned. "But, Mama, I don't like getting my ears cleaned."

"If you don't clean them, potatoes will sprout in there, then how will you hear anything?" Posey teased.

Nate's eyes widened and his index finger immediately went to his ear to make sure nothing had taken root.

"Eat your lunch, honey. I'm going to work on a quilt this afternoon while you do some schoolwork. If you work hard, you can have a break and play with Agnes and Spot later. How does that sound?"

"Good," Nate said, taking the last bite of his sandwich. He tossed a bit of crust to Spot then accepted the cookie Posey handed to him.

Agnes continued parading back and forth across the yard, as though she wanted an audience to see how pretty she looked.

Posey finished her sandwich and wiped her hands on her apron then took Nate's hand in hers. "Come on, son. I have an idea."

Nate skipped along beside her as they walked out to the orchard. Fruit trees, heavy with fragrant, lovely blossoms looked bedecked for a fancy party.

"See all those blossoms on the ground, baby?" Posey knelt beside Nate, pointing to pink and white blossoms covering the ground beneath the trees. "Can you gather up a bunch of those blossoms?"

"Sure, Mama!" Nate laughed as he darted through the orchard with Agnes and Spot chasing after him. He pulled his shirt out of the waist of his pants and used it as a makeshift basket to carry the blossoms back to his mother.

Posey took a seat on the grass in a patch of warm sunshine and pulled an ever-present needle and thread from her apron pocket. She tied a knot in the end of the thread then began stitching the blossoms together.

When she had a length that reached about eighteen inches, she tied the two ends of the thread together, creating a circle of blossoms.

"Whatcha gonna do with that?" Nate asked as he watched her work.

"Since Agnes thinks she is a princess today, we'll give her a crown."

Nate clapped his hands in excitement and hugged the goat as she stood next to him. Posey carefully settled the wreath of flowers over the goat's head. Agnes rolled her eyes up, trying to look at the flowers then regally lifted her head.

Puffed up with pride, the little goat high-stepped her way out of the orchard and made her way to the house, eager to show the kittens her fragrant crown.

"That is the strangest goat," Posey said, rising to her feet and taking Nate's hand in hers.

"Agnes isn't strange, Mama. She's just a girl. Uncle Tad says all girls like to be pretty. Maybe Agnes likes being clean and smelling nice." Nate took a few hops then resumed skipping beside his mother.

"What else does Uncle Tad say about girls?" Posey asked, far more interested in what Tad shared with her son than in any conversation regarding the goat's new infatuation with perfume and flowers.

Nate rubbed a finger over his chin, deep in thought. "Well, he said girls are delicate and I have to be careful not to be too rough with them. And he said girls are just as smart as boys, sometimes smarter. He told me that girls cry sometimes just because."

"I see," Posey said, forcing herself not to smile. Tad had indeed paid attention to girls. "Did he say anything else?"

"Um…" Distracted by a bird sitting on a fence post, Nate stared at it for several seconds before turning back to his mother. "I heard him tell the sheriff that his sister had a steel back covered in lace and ribbons."

"A steel back?" Posey glanced at Nate.

Nate poked Posey along her spine. "I asked him how she got a steel back and he said it was the bone that runs from your neck to your…"

"I get the idea, son." Posey took his hand in hers again as they moseyed toward the house.

"Does his sister really have steel in her back?"

Posey shook her head. "I believe what Tad meant was that his sister is a very strong individual."

Nate took on a dubious expression. "Can she pack big sacks of feed?"

Posey laughed. "Probably not, baby. I didn't refer to physical strength, but moral and mental fortitude."

Nate gave her another confused look then he returned to skipping along beside her. "Uncle Tad said you're strong and beautiful."

Warmed by the thought Tad had said such nice things about her to Nate, Posey smiled. "Oh, he did, did he?"

"Yep. Uncle Tad likes you almost as much as Agnes likes me!" Nate ran ahead, giggling as Agnes marched up and down the porch railing.

"We see you, Agnes, dear, and you look lovely." Posey gave the goat a pat on her back as she walked past her. Quickly gathering their lunch things, Posey washed them while Nate got out his school papers.

Posey opted to work with him at home one more year before she sent him off to school. For an hour or two each day, they worked on numbers and letters. Nate had memorized the entire alphabet. He could also write his name and several simple words, and count up to fifty.

Together, they sat down at the table and spent the next hour going over Nate's spelling words and working on basic math problems.

When the boy could no longer sit still, Posey sent him outside to play. "You and Agnes stay out of trouble."

"Yes, Mama!" Nate hollered as he charged outside and leaped off the porch. Agnes bleated and chased after him as he raced around the yard.

Posey decided to get in a little work on a quilt she was hurrying to finish for Mrs. Owens. The feathered star pattern of dark burgundy on white made quite a striking contrast. She slipped on the leather thimble Tad had made for her a few weeks ago, marveling that he did such kind, thoughtful things for her.

Maybe he really did care for her more than she knew.

Or maybe he thought of her as another sister. She knew he missed his sister, Gloria, even though there was quite an age difference in the two. Perhaps if he'd been around Gloria he would have done similar gestures.

As Posey quilted tiny, even stitches, she let her mind wander from the life she'd built for Nate, with Tad's generous assistance, to the saddle maker who quietly went through his days while giving so much of himself to others.

Many of Tad's characteristics were the same ones she'd admired in John. Yet, the two men were so very different. John never knew a stranger, loved to talk to and tease everyone. While Tad had a playful side, he was much more reserved around people he didn't know well and sometimes around those he did.

Lost in her thoughts, she finally glanced up at the clock on the wall, shocked by how long she'd worked.

Goodness only knew what sort of shenanigans Nate had gotten into outside.

Posey stuck the needle into the fabric, removed her thimble, and rushed outside.

The dog and goat were as conspicuously absent as was Nate.

"Nate? Where are you?" Posey called, walking all around the house and not finding him anywhere. She looked up in the trees to see if he'd somehow managed to climb up one, but they didn't reveal a hiding spot.

She ran out of the yard and over to the barn. A search there didn't reveal her son. He wasn't in the chicken coop, the cellar, the wagon shed, the smokehouse, or outhouse.

Desperate to find him, Posey ran toward the orchard, hoping he'd wandered back there instead of off somewhere else. "Nate! Answer me, baby!"

The only sound she heard was the echo of her own voice on the breeze.

Chapter Six

"I think you'll like this pair better for ranch work," Tad said, handing Thane Jordan a pair of smooth leather gloves from a stack behind the counter.

The rancher tugged them on and flexed his fingers inside the tan leather covering. He spread his fingers then turned over both hands and examined the stitching on the palms.

"These look like they'll have a good bit of wear in them, Palmer. Why don't you add three pairs to that box of supplies?" Thane took off the pair he wore and handed them to Tad.

He added two more pairs of gloves to a box that held saddle cleaning supplies, a braided leather whip Tad had just finished making that morning, and two coils of new rope.

"Is there anything else I can help you with this afternoon, Thane?" Tad asked as he tallied the man's purchases.

"No, I think that'll do it for today." Thane took money from his pocket and handed it to Tad. "How long do you think it'll take you to make those spur straps?"

Tad handed Thane his change and closed the cash register. He glanced down at the notepad where he'd written the custom order for Thane's new spur straps. "As soon as Leroy has the silverwork ready, it shouldn't take me more than a day or so to finish."

Thane nodded his head. "Perfect. He said he should have the silver ready in two weeks." The man looked around Tad's well-stocked store. "Who would have thought when we first moved to town that we'd have so many conveniences here now?"

Tad grinned, recalling the primitive lifestyle many of them endured upon arrival in the area. As they'd matured, the town had also grown. Baker City had much to offer families now, a far cry from its rough days as just a mining town.

"Things have certainly changed."

Thane picked up his box of supplies and headed toward the door. "Thanks, Palmer. See you at church on Sunday."

"I'll be there," Tad said, starting to turn toward his workroom when a long whistle from Thane drew him to a halt.

"What in the..." Thane's words lingered in the air as he gaped out the window.

Tad hurried to the front of the store and threw open the door. The two men stepped outside and watched as Nate Jacobs proudly walked down the street. A flop-eared black and white dog, its bright pink tongue lolling out of its mouth, flanked him on one side while a prancing goat wearing a wreath of flowers around her head kept step on the other.

"Hi, Uncle Tad!" the boy called, waving his hand wildly in the air.

Thane chuckled. "It looks like he stopped by a circus on his way here. Good luck with your very own Pied Piper."

"I'm convinced the goat could have her own act," Tad said quietly, then lifted a departing hand to Thane as the man hurried down the steps and grinned at the boy and his animal pals.

Tad hunkered down and Nate ran up the steps to him, taking a seat on Tad's bent leg. "What brings you to town, Nater?"

"Mama and I gave Agnes a bath and she wanted everyone to see how pretty she looks."

"Agnes or your mama?" Tad teased.

"Agnes!" Nate giggled and placed a hand on the goat's head as it moved in front of them and bleated softly.

"I see you, Miss Agnes, and that is quite a fetching flower arrangement on your head." Tad chuckled when the goat appeared to smile at him, eating up his words of praise.

"Mama made her the crown. She said Agnes gets to be a princess today."

"Is that right?" Tad stood and lifted the boy in his arms then waited as the dog and goat wandered inside his shop. He shut the door and herded them all to the workroom. He pumped a bowl full of water and set it on the floor. The dog slurped at it noisily but the goat took dainty sips, as though she was trying to live up to her temporary royal title.

Tad took a breath and inhaled a perfumed scent that made his thoughts immediately go to Posey. "Did you give the goat a bath with your mama's soap?"

Nate nodded his head, accepting the glass of water Tad gave to him. "Mama wasn't mad, but she told me to use the kitchen soap next time instead of her bath soap. But Agnes smells pretty now, just like Mama."

"Yes, she does," Tad said, taking another breath before realizing how pathetic it was to be so desperate to be closer to Posey that he was inhaling deep whiffs of the goat as a substitute.

Annoyed with himself, Tad picked up Nate and set him on his tall workbench. "What are you and your mama doing today?"

"Mama cleaned the barn and the chicken coop, and we gaved Agnes her bath." Nate took another drink of water then set the glass aside. "Then we had a picnic outside and went to the orchard to get the flowers for Agnes' crown and we sat in the trees and Mama sewed 'em together. You should see the trees, Uncle Tad. They're beautiful! There are white flowers and pink flowers, and they're floating down like fluffy snowflakes!"

"Is that so?" Tad asked, removing the lid from a glass jar on the end of the counter and handed Nate a piece of licorice. The boy eagerly took it and bit off a chunk.

"Thanks, Uncle Tad."

"You're welcome." Tad ruffled his hair. "What else did you do today?"

"Well, me and Mama worked on our numbers and letters. Guess what?" Nate excitedly wiggled back and forth on the bench.

"What? You'll have to tell me or I'll never guess," Tad said, wondering what had Nate so excited.

"I can spell Mama's name and Agnes' name and Spot's name!"

"You can?" Tad feigned a dubious expression. "That's a lot of words for a little boy to know. How about you spell your mama's name for me?"

"Mama is M-A-M-A, but her grown up name is Posey. I can spell it, Uncle Tad. P-O-S-E-Y." Nate beamed. "See! I spelled it!"

"You sure did! That's great, Nate. Good job!" Tad patted the boy on his back then leaned one elbow on the counter, entertained with what excited the youngster. "You'll be the smartest one in your class when you start school next fall."

"Mama says if I keep up my studies, I'll do good." Nate bit off another piece of candy and chewed it.

"What brought you and your mother into town? Is she at the mercantile? You don't usually bring Agnes and Spot with you." Tad watched the boy's face, taken aback by a look he'd seen before, usually when Nate did something he shouldn't.

Nate ducked his head and stared at his feet.

Tad used his forefinger to nudge up the little chin until the boy had to look at him. "Nate? What's going on? Where is your mama?"

Nate shrugged. "At home, I guess. She was working on a quilt when we left."

Tad straightened and stared at the child. "When you left? What do you mean when you left? Did you come into town by yourself? Did you leave without asking her?"

Nate's lip puckered out at Tad's concerned tone and his eyes welled with tears, but he didn't speak.

"Nathaniel John Jacobs! Did you run off without telling your mother where you were going?"

Barely perceptible, Nate's head bobbed up and down.

Tad tamped down the desire to yell at the boy. Losing his temper wouldn't help anything. Instead he picked up the child and held him at eye level. "Nate, it's really important you never leave without telling your mama where you are going. If she tells you no, it's because it's what's best for you. And you shouldn't walk all the way into town by yourself. That's dangerous."

"But Agnes and Spot comed with me and they keeped me safe." Nate's lip quivered and tears threatened to spill. He sniffled and rubbed a hand beneath his nose. "I just wanted you to see how pretty Agnes looks. Spot wanted to show off, too."

Tad patted the child's back comfortingly. "Just promise you will never, ever do something like this again. Your mother is probably worried sick about you."

"Oh, I don't want Mama to worry." Nate squirmed against Tad. As soon as his feet touched the floor, he started to run, but Tad grabbed him in mid-step.

"Where do you think you're going?"

"Home!" Nate said, pushing against Tad to set him down again. "I gotta get home to Mama."

"Just hold your horses, Nater. I'll take you home. Weren't you listening to what I said? It's not safe for you to walk all the way home alone, even if you have Agnes and Spot along. Now, settle down while I lock up the shop and then I'll take you back to your mother."

Nate nodded and quieted. He used the sleeve of his shirt to wipe his nose and face while Tad locked the back door.

He took Nate's little hand in his and led him to the front of the store. A sharp whistle brought the goat and dog racing to the door. "Come on, you three, let's go."

Tad pushed open the door and the boy, goat, and dog raced outside. He locked the door then took Nate's hand in his again and started the walk out to the Jacobs' farm. Posey's place was only about a mile or so from town, but Tad couldn't fathom what had inspired Nate to walk all that way by himself.

Even if he had wanted to show off the goat, he would have thought the little one would have been tuckered out after the trek into Baker City.

They'd only gone a few blocks down Main Street when a cloud of dust signaled a rider racing into town.

Spying them, Posey hauled back on the reins and drew the horse she rode to a sliding stop. Before Tad could do more than blink in surprise, she was off the horse and on her knees in front of her son, hugging him to her while tears streamed down her face.

"Oh, son, I'm so happy to see you." She hugged him so tightly he squirmed for freedom.

"You're smooshing me, Mama!" he finally said, pulling away from her.

Posey ran one hand over his hair while another trailed over his back, making sure her precious boy was in one piece. "Baby, you scared me half to death! What were you thinking, leaving without asking me?"

Nate's lip puckered again. At the worried look on his mother's face, he burst into tears. "I'm sorry, Mama. I didn't mean to be naughty."

He threw himself back in her arms, sobbing against her neck. Posey's tears dripped down her cheeks and fell on the boy's brown head as she held him close.

To add to the rumpus in the middle of the street, the goat and dog crowded close to the boy, pushing against Posey. Tad held the reins of the horse and observed, debating what he could do to help. The dog whined while the goat bleated and tossed her head, sending flower petals dancing into the air.

"Okay, you four, that's enough. I think it's time for someone else to take over as the afternoon entertainment around here," Tad said, grasping Posey's arms in his hands and lifting her to her feet. He took Nate from her and held the boy on one arm while he offered his other to her.

She took it and together, they walked over to the park. Tad got Posey and Nate settled on a bench in the shade then hurried to the drugstore located a few blocks from the park. He returned with three dishes of ice cream.

Nate perked right up at the sight of his treat. While he enthusiastically ate his ice cream, sharing a few bites with Agnes and Spot, Posey spoke quietly to Tad.

"I'm not sure rewarding his bad behavior is a good idea, but who am I to turn down ice cream?"

Tad grinned at her, grateful she'd stopped crying and seemed to be on the way to regaining her good humor. "I think Nate understands what he did was wrong and he won't do it again. He was just so proud of Agnes and wanted to show her off." He chuckled and pointed his spoon at the goat. "I swear she was mincing down the street like she was in a parade."

Posey laughed and the low throaty sound did things to Tad he forced himself to ignore. "She's been acting like the Queen of England since I found Nate giving her a bath. I just hate that he used up all my good soap."

He chuckled and took another bite of his chocolate ice cream. "I bet you have the nicest smelling goat this side of the Rocky Mountains. Maybe even the whole country."

"I don't know about that, but she does smell much better than she has for a long while." Posey gave him a glance from beneath her eyelashes and licked ice cream from her spoon.

Tad's spoon stopped midway to his mouth as he watched her tongue capture the last little bit of creamy confection from her spoon. He wanted, in the worst way, to kiss her lips. He imagined they'd taste sweet, like the caramel-flavored ice cream she ate. Thoughts of her mouth, cool from the frozen treat, warming his skin made gooseflesh ripple over him followed by a delicious shiver.

Mistaking his response to a reaction to the cold ice cream, Posey put a hand on his arm. "Did you eat your ice cream too fast?"

Tad shook his head and hurried to take another bite to keep from answering her. If things continued between the two of them as they had been the last few weeks, Tad had no idea how he'd keep from falling at Posey's feet and confessing his feelings for her.

And that was something he just couldn't do.

Chapter Seven

The bell jangling above his door alerted Tad to a customer. He set down the tool in his hand and hurried into the front of his shop.

His smile broadened as he saw Posey and Nate standing just inside the door.

"What's this? No goat or dog in tow today?" he teased, lifting Nate in his arms when the boy ran to him. He tossed the child in the air twice, eliciting a happy giggle before setting him on the counter.

"The animals remained at home today, but I do have a favor to ask." Posey gave him a long studying glance that left him slightly unsettled. He wondered what she saw when she looked at him that way.

He felt like she could see beyond the surface into his heart where his love for her mingled with the hurts from his past.

Determined not to allow wounds from yesterday to mar the beauty of today, he shoved those thoughts aside and smiled at the lovely woman in front of him.

He noticed she wore the pink dress he'd decided was his new favorite. Everything from the color to the way it glided over her curves accented her desirability. The dark molasses color of her eyes sparkled with an inner light and her lips, those purely perfect kissable pink lips, begged for him to take a taste or two.

Tad blinked and swallowed hard, trying to focus on the words Posey spoke instead of how much he wanted to take her in his arms.

When she fell silent and stared at him expectantly, he knew she'd asked something that required him to respond.

Sheepishly, he grinned at her. "I'm sorry, Posey, I didn't catch what you said."

"I merely asked if you could keep an eye on Nate for a little while. I have a few appointments to attend to then I need to run by the mercantile. If you don't have time to watch him, I'll just take him with me." She moved toward the counter where Nate sat playing with a stack of small square leather pieces hooked together on a sturdy ring. Tad used the samples when he was taking down custom orders.

"Nate can stay here. I don't mind having him in the shop. And take as much time as you need." Tad glanced at the clock. "In fact, if you're finished with your errands in time for lunch, I'd be happy to take you two out to eat."

Posey smiled. "That's so kind of you, Tad, but one of my appointments includes a lunch meeting. I should be back here by half past one. If you don't want to keep Nate that long, just say the word. You can tell me no."

Tad didn't think she realized the error of her statement. He couldn't tell her no, especially when she stood in a shaft of sunlight that turned her hair into a mass of golden curls. Glad she'd removed her hat, he fought down the urge to pull out the pins confining her hair and bury his hands in the shining strands.

By force, he yanked his thoughts back on track and glanced at Nate. "I think Nater can keep me out of trouble for a few hours. Just come back by here when you're ready. There's no hurry or rush." He gave her a long look. "Do you need help with anything, Posey? Is there anything I can do to assist you, other than keep an eye on Nate?"

"No. I have several matters I've put off and want to get them taken care of today. I would have asked Maggie to watch Nate, but she's busy working on gowns for Bella Packwood's upcoming wedding." Posey pinned her hat back on, kissed Nate on his cheek, then tugged on the gloves she'd removed earlier. "You mind Uncle Tad, Nate, and be a good boy while I'm gone."

"Okay, Mama! I'll be good and help Uncle Tad. I'm a good helper!"

Tad chuckled and tweaked Nate's nose then set the boy down from the counter. "Why don't you run into the back and get your apron on, son?"

"Okay!" Nate yelled then raced into the workroom.

"It's so nice of you to make him feel so welcome and special, Tad." Posey placed a hand on his arm and gave it a squeeze.

Even through the fabric of his sleeve and the leather of her glove, he could feel the warmth down to his bones. "Nate is a special boy. You know I care about him a great deal, Posey. Never hesitate to leave him here. You both are always welcome. Always."

She tossed him a sassy grin over her shoulder as she opened the door. "You might not say that after watching Nate for the next several hours. If you need to leave or have a problem, I'll either be at the attorney's office, the bank, or the mercantile."

Frown lines creased Tad's brow as he followed her outside. "Are you sure you don't need me to go with you, Posey. Is everything okay? Why are you..."

She fisted a hand on one hip and stared at him. "Tad Palmer! If you ever want me to speak to you again you will cease treating me as if I'm some helpless female incapable of handling her own affairs. I appreciate you keeping Nate, but if you're going to act like an unduly protective cavedweller, I'll just take him with me."

Tad grinned, amused by her rising temper. "Now, Posey, just calm down. I didn't mean to imply I thought you were helpless, I just wanted to offer my help if you need it."

"Well, I don't." She huffed, then calmed slightly. "But it is kind of you to offer. Thank you. I'll be on my way. Remember, if you have any problems with Nate, just..."

"We'll be fine. I'm not the one who lost him a few weeks ago, now am I?" Tad knew his words goaded her.

She'd started down the boardwalk but stopped and turned around, glaring at him. "I didn't lose him, he ran off. There's a difference, and I'll thank you to never, ever mention that to me again."

She spun around and marched away, her footsteps echoing loudly on the wooden walk.

Energized by their sparring and amused by how easily he ruffled her feathers, Tad returned inside the shop. Nate struggled to tie the strings on the back of a little leather apron Tad had made for the boy to wear when he stayed at the shop with him.

"Here, son, let me do it." Tad lifted up Nate and stood him on top of the front counter. Nate watched over his shoulder as Tad smoothed the straps and then tied the string at his waist. "There you are. All set to work."

"What can I work on, Uncle Tad? Huh? Can I work on some leather? Can I?" Nate wiggled with excitement.

Tad leaned forward and lifted the boy over one brawny shoulder and carried him to the backroom while Nate giggled.

"Uncle Tad?" Nate asked as Tad set him down on the workbench.

"Hmm?"

"Are you the strongest man in the world?"

Tad grinned. "No, Nate. I'm not. There are many, many men much stronger than I am. Why?"

The boy shrugged and picked up a scrap piece of leather, rubbing it between his thumb and finger. "I dunno. It's just you're so strong and you take good care of us. I think Mama likes those things." The boy pointed to the muscles visible beneath the cloth of Tad's shirt.

Tad glanced down at his chest and then his arms. "Likes what?"

Nate reached out and poked the curve of muscle at Tad's shoulder. "Those. She watches them when you work at our house. Will I have those someday?"

Well, well. That was an interesting tidbit. Tad didn't rightly care if Nate turned his shop inside out and backwards. Any mess the boy made would be worth it just to discover Posey watched his muscles while he worked. If even a five-year-old noticed her interest in him, what else had Tad missed?

Did Posey really care for him as she would a man that piqued her interest, not one she looked at as a brother?

What would he do about it if she did? Could he betray John's memory and all the man's friendship meant to him by admitting he loved Posey?

Torn between what his heart wanted and what he felt he owed his friend, Tad set to work on a saddle Tully Barrett special-ordered.

He gave Nate a scrap piece of leather and a dull-edged knife then convinced the boy he'd be a big help in smoothing the leather by rubbing it with the knife.

An hour later, Tad bent over a piece of leather he skived. He felt warm breath on his hand and glanced up to find Nate intently watching his every move.

"Whatcha doing, Uncle Tad?"

Tad continued working, but shifted so Nate could get a better view of the way he cut the leather. "This is called skiving, Nate."

"What's that do?" the little boy asked, inquisitive as he observed Tad's movements.

"Skiving is how I reduce the thickness of leather, especially in areas that will be bent or folded. It has to be pliable without becoming weak."

"What's pliable mean, Uncle Tad?" Nate held his hands together, as though he didn't trust himself not to reach out and touch something.

"Pliable?" Tad asked.

Nate nodded and continued watching.

"Pliable means that something bends or moves easily. It yields to the forces around it."

"Oh," Nate said, absorbing the explanation. The boy stared across the room and pointed to the candy jar. "Like licorice! Is it pliable, Uncle Tad?"

"That's right, Nater. You've got the idea."

"Do you think I could have some pliable licorice?" the boy asked.

Tad laughed. "You are a schemer, Nate Jacobs. And the answer to your question is not right now. We'll eat lunch soon. Then, if you still want some later, you can have a piece."

"Okay," Nate said, without any argument.

The bell rang above the door, so Tad set down his tools, lifted Nate down and the two of them went to greet his customer. After Tad helped Ian McGregor choose a new pair of gloves and sold the man a pair of hobbles, he and Nate went upstairs to his living quarters to eat lunch.

Tad fried bacon and eggs then toasted a few slices of bread and made them both sandwiches. A can of peaches and glasses of milk rounded out their meal.

"You cook good, Uncle Tad," Nate said as he bit into a piece of crispy bacon. "Mama cooks good, too. I like good food."

Tad nodded in agreement. "So do I, Nater." He leaned closer to the little boy and dropped his voice conspiratorially. "I'll tell you a secret, though."

Nate's eyes rounded and he stared at Tad. "What kind of secret?"

"Well, when I was growing up, I didn't know how to cook anything. Neither did my mother nor my sister. To this day, I don't think Gloria could fry an egg if she had to."

"Really? Does your dad cook for them?" Nate took another bite of his sandwich.

"No, my father doesn't cook either. They have people who cook for them, although Gloria's husband might be able to cook. I haven't actually asked him. He's a talented composer, though."

Nate's little forehead wrinkled in thought. "What's a poser?"

"A composer?"

Nate nodded and took a gulp of his milk. "Yeah. What's that?"

"A composer writes music. You've seen the music the pianist at church plays, haven't you, or the music I sometimes use when I fiddle?"

"Yep!"

"Well, those lines and dots on the paper are notes and someone with far more talent than I could hope to possess arranges them in a way that makes music."

"Oh, that's neat, Uncle Tad." Nate reached across the table and patted his hand. "But you do good stuff, too. You make the nicest, bestest saddles. Everyone says so. Mama said peoples come from all over just to buy your saddles. When I grow up, I'm gonna make saddles with you. Will that be okay,

Uncle Tad? That way, I'll get to see you every day and we can have bacon for lunch all the time!"

Tad chuckled and ruffled Nate's unruly hair. "I think that's a grand idea, Nater."

Lunch continued with a lively discussion about Spot and Agnes, the vegetables sprouting in Posey's garden, and the pony Nate decided he wanted.

Tad figured the boy got into enough trouble without adding a pony to the mix, but eventually he needed to learn to ride. He'd offered several times to give Nate lessons, but Posey always refused.

An accomplished rider in her own right, Tad assumed Posey would teach Nate to ride when she felt her son was ready, or when she was ready to allow him the freedom and responsibility it would offer.

He finished his sandwiches and peaches, and then leaned back in his chair, drinking his milk. Nate bit down on a piece of particularly crispy bacon and screamed.

Tad thumped the glass on the table with such force, the glass tipped over and the remaining milk pooled across the surface.

In a blink, he was on his knees next to Nate's chair, the boy's arms held in his hands as he searched his face, trying to divine what caused him pain. "What's wrong, son? What happened? What hurts?"

"My tooth," Nate whimpered. Tad grabbed a dish towel and held it in front of Nate's mouth while the boy spit into it. A little white tooth shone from amid pieces of bacon.

Tad grinned and held the tooth in his fingers. "Well, Nater, you just lost your first tooth."

The boy's eyes widened and he looked frightened as he stuck a finger in his mouth, touching the space in the bottom front where his tooth used to be.

"Will all my teeth fall out? Will I look like Mr. Bentley?" Panic edged the boy's voice as he turned teary eyes to Tad.

He pulled the youngster into a hug then set him back on his chair. "Didn't your mama tell you about baby teeth and big boy teeth?"

Nate shook his head, fingering the gap in his teeth again. Tad pulled his finger away and held a rag to the spot on the youngster's gums that slightly bled.

"All the teeth you have right now are what we call baby teeth, Nate. And for the next few years all those teeth with fall out, one at a time, and new teeth will come in to take their place. When you get all done, you'll have big boy teeth, like mine." Tad smiled broadly so Nate could see all his large, even teeth.

"Will mine look like yours and Mama's?"

"Most likely," Tad said, thinking of the white pearl-like teeth that made up Posey's lovely smile.

"Can I show Mama my tooth?" Nate asked, taking the little tooth off Tad's palm and looking at it.

"You sure can. I think we should put it in something so it doesn't get lost before she comes back." Tad stood and dug around until he found a small jar. He set the tooth inside and fastened on the lid, so Nate didn't accidentally lose it. He had an idea Posey would want to keep the little tooth until she was old and gray. He was pretty sure she'd never forgive him if he lost it on his watch.

Once Nate calmed down and decided it was a great thing to have lost his tooth, he and Tad returned downstairs. While Tad continued skiving leather, Nate took the broom and swept it around the floor in the workroom. There wasn't anything there he could damage with his wild sweeping motions. Tad kept one eye on the boy and one on his work as he awaited Posey's arrival.

At precisely half past one, the bell above the door jingled. Tad and Nate rushed to the front of the store and almost collided with Posey as she made her way toward the back.

A look of fury rode her face and she held herself stiffly as she glared at Tad.

With no idea what he'd done to raise her ire, he snatched the jar with the tooth off the front counter and shoved it into her hands.

She stared at it then Nate started jabbering about losing his tooth in his bacon and it being the best lunch he ever had and Tad being a great cook.

"You lost your tooth? Your first tooth?" Posey bent down and tugged on Nate's chin until he opened his mouth, showing off the gap where his tooth had once been.

She looked from Nate to Tad with tears glistening in her eyes. "He lost his first tooth and I wasn't even here to see it." She stood and closed her eyes, drew in a deep breath, gathering her composure before she smiled at Nate. "It's very exciting, isn't it, baby?"

"Oh, yes, Mama. And Tad said sometimes you get a coin under your pillow in exchange for your tooth from magical fairies. Do you think there will be magical fairies at our house, Mama?"

"I don't know. We'll have to see, won't we, sweetheart. Run get your cap, baby, and we'll head home. I'm sure Agnes misses you." Posey waited until Nate scampered into the workroom before turning to Tad with an unsettling mixture of gratitude and anger.

"I can tell you're mad about something, but I don't know what I've done, so you'll have to explain it to me," he said, keeping his voice low.

"We'll speak of it another day." Posey placed a hand on his arm.

The warmth of it made tingles zoom all the way to his head and toes at the slight contact. He nodded in agreement, uncertain he could speak with his thoughts all in a jumble, most of them wondering what she'd do if he pulled her to him and kissed her. With irritation lending color to her cheeks and a flame to her eyes, he found her nearly irresistible.

Given her current agitated state, though, he decided it best not to test her patience further.

"Thank you for taking such good care of Nate, Tad. I appreciate you watching him, and for making losing his tooth something fun. I'll be sure to slip a coin or two beneath his pillow."

"Do you need some coins? I can give you…" He started to dig into his pocket, but she squeezed his arm.

"That isn't necessary, Tad. I'll handle it, just as I thought I'd been handling things all along."

Baffled by her cryptic statement, Tad wisely kept his questions to himself and walked Posey and Nate out when the boy raced back into the room with his cap and a picture he'd drawn on a piece of paper Tad used to sketch out patterns.

"What did you draw, baby?" Posey asked, bending down to look at his drawing when they stepped outside.

"It's you and me and Agnes and Spot and the kitties and Tad. It's my family. All the people I love." Nate beamed at Posey as he pointed out each blob in his picture. Tad had noticed various sizes of shapes and thought one might have resembled the goat, but had no idea what the little boy drew.

Tad hunkered down and placed a hand on Nate's shoulder. "I'm sure happy you include me as part of your family, Nater. I love you, son."

"I love you, too, Uncle Tad. Thank you for letting me stay with you and for saving my tooth." Nate hugged him back then turned to his mother. "I almost ate it, Mama! It was crunchy like my bacon."

"My goodness!" she said. "We best hurry right home so you can show it to Agnes and Spot."

"Yep!" Nate giggled as Tad swung him up on the wagon seat.

Rather than give Posey a hand, Tad swung her up, much as he had Nate, trying not to laugh at the shocked expression on her face.

She reached up to right her hat that listed to one side then straightened her skirts before pinning him with a scowl, clearly disconcerted. "Thank you, Mr. Palmer. Good day."

Amused by her discombobulated state, he chuckled as she snapped the reins and drove away, taking his heart with her.

Chapter Eight

A week passed before Posey worked up the nerve to confront Tad about the matter that had left her so infuriated the day Nate lost his tooth.

If it hadn't been for that, she might have lambasted Tad the moment she set foot in his shop. As it was, after taking Nate home and talking all about what to expect as he lost his baby teeth, she was no longer in the mood to ream Tad's ears.

However, the longer she put off having a discussion with the man, the more her stomach churned and anxiety gnawed at her. Avoidance wouldn't make the need to talk to him go away, so she took Nate into town with her, begged Maggie to keep an eye on him, and marched over to the saddle shop.

When she walked inside, the sheriff and Tad laughed over a joke one of them must have told. At her appearance, they both sobered and turned her way.

Tully doffed his hat and Tad politely tipped his head to her.

"Afternoon, Posey," Tad said, smiling at her. After her cool response to him following church services Sunday, he probably wondered why she'd come to see him. "What brings you into town?" He glanced around her, expecting her son to race inside at any moment. "Where's Nate?"

"He's visiting Maggie right now," Posey said, avoiding looking at Tad as her gaze swept around his shop.

Mindful of the sudden tension lingering in the air, Tully cleared his throat. "Well, I reckon I'll head over there and check on him. With Maggie, she's liable to stick him in a dress and pin ribbons in his hair if we aren't careful," he teased and then turned back to Tad. "The saddle looks good. I can't wait to try it out as soon as you finish it."

"I'll have it ready in a few days, Tully," Tad said, absently watching Posey's every move.

Tully studied them both a moment before snickering softly and wandering out the door.

Tad moved around the counter and stood in front of Posey.

Unsettled by his proximity and the enticing, manly scent of him, she took a step back and bumped into one of the display saddles.

"Careful, Posey Jo," Tad said in a low, husky voice, reaching out a hand and pulling her forward.

Ripples of delight shot through her, but she ignored them, bringing her focus back to the reason for coming to see Tad.

"We need to talk. Would it be okay to go into your workroom?" she asked, tipping her head toward the doorway to the back room.

"Certainly," Tad said, motioning for her to precede him.

She could feel his eyes on her as she walked across the store, but didn't falter in her steps or glance back at him. In the workroom, she set her reticule on a workbench and removed her gloves and hat, tossing them down, too. For the length of several heartbeats, she studied Tad. The dark blue shirt he wore made his eyes look even bluer. As usual, his short hair was tousled with a few strands feathered around his face. Despite the growth of stubble along his square jaw, he owned a boyish appearance that made it hard for her to hold onto her anger against him.

Tad Palmer was undeniably attractive. It wasn't just his broad shoulders and muscular form that appealed to her, either. He went through his days with a quiet, unassuming strength many relied on. Kind and generous, he was also loyal and dependable. The combination of those last four traits were the reason she'd gotten so ridiculously angry the other day.

"What's going on, Posey?" Tad asked, motioning for her to take a seat on one of the tall stools at his worktable.

She shook her head and firmed her resolve to speak what was on her mind, even if she refused to give voice to what was on her heart. "Tad Palmer! I can't believe you've lied to me since John's passing. How could you do that?"

Stunned by her accusation, Tad merely stared at her in mute surprise.

"Don't you pretend to be innocent. I know all about what you did." She took a step closer to him, holding his gaze with her irate glare. "The other day I was doing some spring cleaning. I found a box of papers, things John had kept that I'd never worried about looking into. After going through them, I went to see Mr. Dylan, the attorney."

"Yeah, you mentioned that last week, but what's that got to do with me?" Tad took a seat on a stool, watching Posey pace back and forth in front of him.

"It has everything to do with you, and you know it!" She stamped her foot in frustration. "Why didn't you tell me the truth, Tad? Why?"

"About…?"

"The Limitless!" She spat out, infuriated. "You let me think John was the sole owner when you were his partner all along. When you sold the mine on my behalf, you gave me every single penny. Half of it was rightfully yours." She crossed her arms over her chest and glared at him. "From the papers I found, your share was more like two thirds because you'd invested heavily in the mine. You couldn't afford to do that, Tad. You live in that tiny apartment upstairs and work such long, hard hours to make ends meet. The money that has kept Nate and I living comfortably is really yours!"

"No, Posey. It's yours. I couldn't have lived with myself if I hadn't made sure you and Nate were taken care of."

"But we weren't your responsibility or problem, Tad. And we owe you, so much." Her arms fell to her sides and she took a step closer to him.

A soft light shone from his eyes as he reached out and took her hand in his. The gentle way he rubbed his thumb across her palm made fiery currents flow from her fingers to her toes.

"Posey, I made John a promise to take care of his girl and I intend to keep it. I didn't need the money from the sale of the mine, but you and Nate did. And you have never been a problem. Helping you has been my honor and pleasure."

The anger melted out of her at the sincere look on his face. "You shouldn't have let me continue thinking John was the sole owner of the mine, though. Haven't you ever heard of a lie by omission?"

He grinned. "I have and admittedly it was, but if I'd told you the truth, you wouldn't have accepted the money. You needed it. I hate that you work so hard making quilts and seeing to things at your place as it is. If you'd let me, I'd do more for you."

She shook her head. "I'm not some weakling incapable of taking care of herself or her son, Tad. I enjoy making my quilts and I like to work outside on our little farm. It's good for Nate to help, too. And somehow, someday, I intend to pay back every cent I owe you. If you want your money now, I have some money tucked away I can give you."

Tad shook his head and subtly pulled Posey closer. "I don't want or need your money. I've got more than enough of my own."

She gave him a dubious look and waved one hand around his shop. "That's why you live such a simple life? Because you've money to spare. Don't be ludicrous, Tad."

He shrugged. "I'm not. Look, Posey, I suppose while you're in the mood to discover all my secrets, you might as well learn one more. I don't need money. I truly do have enough of my own."

"What are you talking about?" She drew back and stared at him.

"Remember when I told you a long time ago that my family had some money but I wanted no part of it?"

She nodded.

"Well, that is true. I left home without taking a dime of my parents' money. My parents own Davis Shipping in Virginia. My mother was a Davis and Father took over the business from my grandparents." He sighed and ran a hand over his head, further mussing his hair. "My grandparents left a trust fund for my sister and me. I received the funds when I turned twenty-three. That's the money I used to help buy the mine. And that's why I don't need your money, Posey. I could close this shop and never work another day in my life, and still have plenty."

"Oh, I had no idea." She wondered how Tad could live such a humble existence. Surely he'd grown up amid luxuries, surrounded by great wealth.

As though he could read her mind, he smiled. "I don't miss all the falderol of living in my parents' fancy home. I like it here, like my life and my friends. I wouldn't trade it for anything, although Gloria does think I should at least have running water installed in my apartment. She's warned me if she and Colin ever come to visit, she'll stay at the hotel rather than with me."

"She's a very smart girl," Posey said, giving him a teasing look.

Disturbed by the odd light glowing in his eyes and the determined look on his face, she didn't even think of resisting. Not when her gaze fixated on his lips and how much she wanted to taste his kiss.

Unable to recall when Tad's mouth had first fascinated her, all she knew was for the last two years, she'd dreamed of him taking her in his arms and kissing her with the same level of passion he stirred in her.

In spite of the lingering guilt she felt about falling in love again, she knew John would be glad the one who'd captured her heart was Tad. Her husband had often said there was no one finer than his best friend, and Posey heartily agreed.

"I never wanted or needed your money, Posey Jo," Tad growled, slowly lowering his head toward hers as he continued to draw her closer. He sat on the stool with his legs bracketing her on either side. "What I want..." One of his big hands slid around to cup the back of her head while the other encircled her waist. "Is to kiss you."

Warmth flooded through Posey and her lips curved upward in a smile. "Why, then, are you still talking instead of kissing me?"

Hesitantly, Tad's lips moved over hers in a light caress.

Thrilled with the scrumptious euphoria created by finally being in the place she'd longed for so long, Posey slid her hands up his arms and rested them on his broad shoulders, moving nearer to him.

Tad moaned and deepened the kiss, wrapping both arms around her as he took possession of her mouth and laid claim to her soul.

Consumed with the passion arcing between them, Posey wouldn't have been able to break away from

Tad in that moment if the building had collapsed around them. Her only thought was that it felt so good, so right, to be in Tad's arms.

His kisses, rich and dark, filled her with a yearning she never again thought to experience. As he lavished her with his affection, something that had long rested dormant in her heart burst into full bloom.

Oh, how she loved this good, kind, caring man. A man full of secrets and complexities that she'd never imagined. Not her Tad.

Wholly given to the experience of his kisses, to the wonder of being held so lovingly in his arms, Posey sucked in a gulp of astonishment when Tad suddenly pulled back and got to his feet, moving away from her.

"This isn't right, Posey. I'm sorry. I shouldn't have... it's wrong to..."

She sidled up to him and wrapped her arms around his lean waist, pressing against him. "It's okay, Tad. There's nothing wrong in..."

"Yes, there is." He pushed her away again and moved so he stood on the other side of the worktable. "I'm sorry I didn't tell you the whole truth, Posey, and I'm really sorry about kissing you. It won't happen again."

"Well, perhaps I want it to." She gave him a look that caused him to swallow hard as his gaze focused on her just-kissed mouth. "Maybe there's nothing I'd like better than for you to kiss me repeatedly."

"Posey, no. You're just caught up in the moment and confused." He plopped her hat on her head, shoved her gloves and reticule into her hands, and took her elbow in his hand. In a rush, he escorted her to the front of the store. "I'm sorry, but I can't do this, Posey. Goodbye."

He nudged her out the door and closed it behind her.

Posey yanked on her gloves with a jerk. "That man is the most thick-headed, stubborn fool I've ever encountered," she muttered as she marched down the boardwalk. "We'll just see about him never kissing me again."

Chapter Nine

"He did what?" Maggie asked, eyes wide with disbelief as Posey sat at her kitchen table, relaying what had transpired with Tad.

"He threw me out of his shop!" Posey huffed and stirred more sugar into her cup of tea. Affronted, shamed, and downright infuriated, she didn't know which emotion to give full rein first and wavered between all three. Although she left out Tad's confession to having a healthy bank account, she did tell Maggie about him kissing then rejecting her. "Stupid, stupid man!"

"Men can be such thoughtless, brainless creatures," Maggie said, reaching across the table and patting Posey on the arm. "Why, my Daniel could do and say the most idiotic things then wonder why he got cold, lumpy porridge for supper."

Posey sighed. "Tad's so mule-headed that he rarely even comes to share a meal with us lately. You'd think Nate and I had the plague or some such thing for as hard as he works to stay away from us."

At the sound of his name, Nate ran into Maggie's kitchen from where he'd played in her sitting room with a set of blocks. "May I have a cookie, Miss Maggie?" the boy asked sweetly.

"Of course, young man. You sit right there by your mama," Maggie said, pointing to a chair. She poured him a glass of milk and put two cookies in a plate, setting it before him before she resumed her seat.

"Did you see Uncle Tad, Mama?" Nate asked innocently.

"I sure did, baby."

"Is he still working on the sheriff's saddle?" Nate looked to his mother as he took a bite of cookie.

Posey nodded. "He is, honey. I heard him tell the sheriff he'll have it finished soon. Is that the saddle you helped him work on?"

"Yep! I helped good." Nate took another bite then a big gulp of milk.

Maggie grinned at the little boy. "My goodness, I didn't realize you helped Mr. Palmer in his shop. We'll have to be sure to tell Sheriff Barrett that his saddle is extra special because you've been helping with it."

Nate beamed and nodded his head, making his hair flop forward.

Posey smiled and brushed it away from his face.

Later, after she'd thanked Maggie for watching Nate and the delicious refreshments, they stood at Maggie's back door. Nate tried to get close to an alley cat sunning itself a few yards away.

SHANNA HATFIELD

"It seems to me Tad is fighting his feelings for you, Posey. You could give him a little competition, make him jealous."

"I couldn't do that, even if there was someone who'd pretend to show interest in me."

Maggie shrugged. "You could make it impossible for him to ignore you. Invite him over for supper and make sure you're very attentive to him. That used to work quite well with Daniel when I wanted to get his attention."

Posey smiled then shook her head. "I don't think so. I wouldn't want him to get the wrong idea."

"What idea would that be? That you're a beautiful, available woman who has eyes only for him?" Maggie laughed. "Even if he's too blind to see it, the rest of us have noticed. We've made note of the way he can't take his eyes off you, too."

"I think you and those others you mentioned might want to swing by Doc's office and have your vision checked," Posey teased then motioned to Nate.

"Come along, son. Time to go home." She turned back to Maggie. "Thank you, again, for watching him. If there's anything I can do for you, just let me know."

"It was my pleasure, Posey. Anytime you need someone to keep an eye on Nate, let me know."

"I might just do that." Posey took her son's hand in hers and moved a few steps down the alley. "Thank you, Maggie."

Maggie waved. "It was my pleasure. It's not every day a lively boy wants to spend time in my dress shop."

Chapter Ten

Tad straightened from his bent over position above his workbench and stretched his back. He'd spent the last hour meticulously stamping a piece of leather that would end up on the skirt of a saddle for Luden Scott. The man was a wonder with horses and ran a successful training business a few miles out of town.

The intricate details on the saddle Luden ordered proved a welcome challenge for Tad. He needed something to occupy his thoughts besides Posey.

Since he'd so stupidly kissed her, he couldn't think of anything else. He'd barely slept a wink and had lost five pounds from being too distracted to eat.

He'd also ruined more leather in the last week from failing to pay attention to what he was doing than he'd done in the rest of his life combined.

Something had to be done to chase thoughts of the woman from his head, but he had no idea what. The notion of turning his attention to another woman wasn't even a consideration.

He loved Posey. Loved her to the very depths of his heart and soul, even if he'd never admit it to her.

Frustrated and flustered, he set aside his tools and decided to close his shop long enough to run down to the hotel's dining room. With as many meals as he'd missed recently, he figured he deserved to indulge in one of the hotel's fine meals. Maybe he'd even order dessert. He'd yet to eat one of their sweet offerings that wasn't incredibly tasty.

After removing his work apron and washing his hands, Tad settled a hat on his head and locked his shop doors.

In no rush to return to work, he ambled down the boardwalk, glancing in store windows and noticing the bright blue sky overhead.

Before long, summer heat would beat down on them with ruthless force, making the area residents long for spring or autumn weather.

It had been quite a change for Tad when he left behind his home in Virginia and traveled west to this land dotted with sagebrush and not much else. Majestic mountains towered in the distance, where many men, like John, had worked hard to make a living in the mines.

Years of growing accustomed to the harsh winters and scorching summers had left Tad glad he'd made Baker City his home. He loved the area and felt true kinship to many of the people who lived in the community.

Although no one had filled the vacancy in his life left by John's death, Tad counted several men among his good friends.

He liked the Scottish man who took over the lumberyard. Ian McGregor was a fun-loving sort who worked and played hard. He'd give the shirt off his back to anyone who needed it and never ask for anything in return.

Thane Jordan was another man he liked and admired. Like Tad and John, Thane had arrived in Baker City young and green. He'd worked in a mine with Maggie's husband and Tully Barrett. Once he made enough to venture out on his own, Thane started buying land and building up his ranch. The man owned a handful of mines and thousands of acres, along with a fine herd of beef cattle and several thoroughbred horses.

One of these days he might have to take Thane up on his offer to come out and visit the Jordan Ranch to see the most recent improvements on the place. It had been a few months since he'd been out to the place, although he used to visit more often.

The sheriff rode out there with some frequency. Perhaps, the next time Tully went, he would tag along. Despite the sheriff's tendency to tease and joke, sometimes without mercy, Tad liked Tully. He was a fair man, and an honest one. He was another one who'd lay down his life for his friends, or fight to protect them until his last breath.

Tad smiled. Those were the kind of friends that many people went a whole lifetime without knowing and he'd had the pleasure of knowing several.

Even Maggie's husband, Daniel, had been someone Tad considered a friend right up until the man's unfortunate death. He was glad Thane and Tully kept an eye on his widow. Between the two of them, he didn't think there was much lacking in Maggie's world, other than the love of a good man.

He'd seen the pain that lingered in Maggie's eyes just like he'd noticed it in Posey's. It shone brightly from Maggie's, though he'd noticed it had dimmed considerably in Posey's, especially the last few months.

Tad stopped in the middle of the street as a thought struck him. What if Posey had found love again? What if some man, someone other than him, had made her smile? Something, or someone, had definitely added pink blossoms to her cheeks and a spring to her step.

Sure, he'd noticed she'd found happiness in life again. That she tended to hum happy tunes while she worked in the kitchen and around the yard. He couldn't help but observe the warmth shining in her gorgeous brown eyes or the welcoming smile on her delectable lips.

Lips that he'd kissed quite thoroughly just last week.

As his thoughts rolled back around to Posey and how much he'd enjoyed kissing her, how much he wanted to do it every day for the rest of his life, he forced his mind to think of something else. Anything else.

Quickly crossing the street, he was absorbed in working on a new saddle pattern in his head as he walked past the hotel dining room's windows.

His jaw dropped open and his feet rooted to the boardwalk as he stared at Posey eating lunch with Tully Barrett.

The sheriff said something that made her laugh. She leaned forward and playfully tapped his arm with a fan she held in one hand.

Tad might not know a lot about women, but he recognized blatant flirtation when he observed it.

Incensed, he clenched his fists at his sides, battling the desire to march inside and bust Tully square in his nose.

Rather than surrender to the urge, Tad gave the couple one last look and stalked down the street. With no direction in mind, he'd reached Ian's lumberyard before he realized how far he'd gone.

When Ian lifted a hand in friendly greeting, Tad waved and turned around, walking back into town and heading straight to the livery where he kept his horses.

He stepped inside the cool shadows of the livery and tipped his head in greeting to the owner. "Milt, I need Licorice."

The livery owner grinned and pointed toward the door. "Head right on down to the mercantile. Frank Miller always has a nice assortment of sweets."

Tad glared at him. "I knew I shouldn't have named that horse after a piece of candy."

Milt laughed. "It does make for some funny jokes."

Tad lifted the horse's halter from a peg on the wall and opened the stall door. "Hey, boy. Want to go for a run?"

The horse tossed his head, eager for fresh air and a chance to run.

"What brings you out in the middle of the day? It's usually evening when you come by to give this fellow an opportunity to stretch his legs." The livery owner settled a blanket over the back of the horse and smoothed it out.

"I just needed a break, that's all." Tad lifted his saddle onto the back of the horse. With easy, practiced movements, he tightened the cinch and was soon leading Licorice outside. The big gelding's black coat glistened in the afternoon sunlight.

"Well, enjoy your ride. A few more weeks, it'll start getting too hot to do much of anything in the middle of the day besides sweat and complain."

"That's for sure," Tad agreed. He swung into the saddle in a smooth motion. "I'm not sure what time I'll be back, but I'll see to putting him away."

"If I'm already gone for the evening, you know where to find the key." Milt waved a hand as Tad turned the horse and started down the street.

He kept Licorice to a walk until they hit the outskirts of Baker City. Rather than ride out of town, Tad made his way to the cemetery. He left Licorice tied to the fence and somberly walked between the headstones until he stood at John Jacobs' grave.

After a hard swallow, he dropped down to his knees and pulled a few straggly weeds trying to sprout around the heavy stone.

"I know I haven't been by to visit for a while, John," Tad said, speaking aloud. He was the only one in the cemetery, otherwise he would have remained silent. "Posey and Nate are both doing well. She's been busy working on her quilts and Nate is growing like a weed. He's such a clever little rascal. You'd be so proud of them both."

Tad gathered the weeds into a little pile then stared at the headstone. "I feel like I should confess to you, John, that I'm in love with your wife. I have been for a while. I mean, I wasn't when you were alive, but sometime between helping her over her grief and watching her smile again I fell in love with her. I didn't mean to. Didn't plan on it. But don't worry, I don't plan to do anything about it. You know my mother and Arabella cured me of ever contemplating marriage, even to a woman as fine as Posey."

He rose to his feet and picked up the weeds. "I sure miss you, John. We all do."

Abruptly, he turned and made his way back to Licorice. He found Pastor Eagan standing there, petting the horse.

Tad tossed aside the weeds, brushed his hands on his trousers, and then shook hands with the pastor. "What are you doing out here, Pastor?"

"Oh, I was just out for a stroll and happened to notice Licorice waiting here at the gate." The pastor gave the horse a final pat then studied Tad. "Are you doing okay, son? You look like you have heavy thoughts weighing on your mind."

Tad shrugged. "I'm fine, sir, but thank you for asking."

"Well, if you ever want to talk, my door is always open."

With a non-committal nod, Tad took Licorice's reins in his hands and fell into step beside Pastor Eagan as the man made his way back toward town.

"You know, I had a few conversations with John over the years, when things were bothering him." The pastor gave Tad another studying glance. "The one thing that never changed with him was that he always valued and treasured the gifts he'd been given."

At Tad's interested, yet confused look, the pastor smiled and continued. "John once told me that he didn't care if his mine never produced an ounce of gold or if it produced millions of dollars worth, he had all the treasure he needed in his wife and son. I always thought John was a particularly smart man, one who knew how to be grateful for the unexpected gifts sent his way."

Tad narrowed his gaze as he stared at the pastor. "If there's something you think I need to know or hear, Pastor, please just spit it out."

Pastor Eagan chuckled and thumped a hand on Tad's shoulder. "Oh, son, some things you have to figure out for yourself. But it wouldn't hurt for you to consider what I said about your friend. He'd want both you and Posey to be happy."

The pastor shoved his hands in his pockets and strode off, whistling a rousing rendition of "Rock of Ages." He glanced back once, grinning at Tad with a knowing look on his face.

Tad watched him go then mounted Licorice and reined the horse around, heading away from town. Although he'd hoped a visit to the cemetery would somehow give him a measure of peace, he felt even more upset and confused.

In no hurry to return to his shop and the thoughts that plagued him, he rode past the last of the buildings near Baker City then gave the horse his head and let him gallop down the road.

Puffs of dust kicked up from the horse's hooves and floated in the air behind them while the pounding gait echoed in the air and Tad's ears.

No matter how fast or far he rode, he still couldn't get thoughts of Posey out of his head. He kept seeing her sitting across from Tully, fully wrapped up in whatever it was the sheriff said to her. When had she started seeing him? Had it been before or after Easter? Why hadn't she mentioned anything? Why had she so fully participated in his kisses the other day if she was seeing the sheriff? If she was playing some sort of game, it wouldn't end well. Of that much, he was certain.

Angry and annoyed, Tad knew he had no right to be. He had no claim on Posey. None at all. If she wanted to date every eligible man in Baker City, he had no reason to complain.

However, thoughts of anyone else even thinking about kissing her made him so irate he bit his lip until he tasted blood.

Tumultuous thoughts coupled with outlandish visions of men pursuing Posey left him so unreasonable and distraught, he missed seeing the coiled snake in the road until he was practically on top of it.

Frightened, Licorice veered around it and bucked a few times. Unprepared for the horse's sudden actions, Tad flew through the air and landed with a thud in the powdery dust a few feet from the snake.

Convinced it would strike before he could reach for his pistol, Tad suddenly remembered he hadn't taken time to strap on his gun belt before he stormed out of town.

With slow movements, he moved backward while the snake's rattles filled the air with an eerie, unpleasant sound. Its head bobbed slightly, forked tongue flickering as it focused a beady gaze on him.

The horse whinnied and danced behind Tad. "It's okay, boy. Just calm down." He spoke in a low, soothing tone, hoping the horse didn't decide to bolt and leave him on foot miles from nowhere.

Tad painstakingly inched away from the reptile until he was out of striking distance. The snake continued rattling his tail, but no longer appeared volatile. Expelling the breath he'd been holding, Tad took Licorice's reins in his hands and led the horse several feet down the road before he mounted and continued on his way.

Although he left town without a destination in mind, he decided since he was nearly there to ride out to Thane Jordan's ranch.

He topped a hill then followed the lane that led down to the ranch yard where Thane lived in a small cabin and his crew shared a large bunkhouse. Various outbuildings gave the place a prosperous feeling, even if it lacked a proper home.

Tad waved as two dogs barked and a lone figure stepped out of the barn. The man raised a hand in greeting. Thane Jordan smiled as Tad drew Licorice to a halt and swung out of the saddle. He took the man's outstretched hand and shook it.

"What brings you all the way out here?" Thane asked, opening the corral gate for Tad to lead the horse inside. Licorice could nibble on feed or drink from the water trough there while Tad spoke with Thane.

"I just needed some fresh air and time to think," Tad admitted as he followed Thane inside the barn.

The man appeared to be repairing a stall, so Tad held one end of a board while Thane tapped nails into the other end.

"You rode all the way out here just to think and breathe in fresh air?" Thane gave him a curious glance then tapped in another nail.

"Something like that." Tad knew Thane was best friends with Tully Barrett. Part of him wanted to question the man about Tully's intentions toward Posey. He must have intentions, or else he wouldn't have been eating lunch with her at the hotel's dining room. From what he glimpsed in the window, the two of them certainly seemed cozy and friendly.

Undeniably upset at seeing Posey with another man, Tad hadn't even given a thought to what the woman had done with Nate? Had she left him at Maggie's again? Had she found someone new to watch the boy?

He missed the days when she'd bring him to his shop. Despite the messes and inevitable trouble Nate got into, Tad liked having him around, underfoot. Inquisitive and bright, Nate filled the quiet in the shop with his happy chatter. Tad enjoyed seeing the world from the youngster's perspective or listening to the boy's explanations of how he thought things worked.

For an hour, Tad helped Thane until the stall looked like new. When they finished, Thane wiped off his tools and stored them in a large case, then turned to Tad. "Do you want to tell me why you're really here? If all you wanted was fresh air, there's an abundance of it most anywhere around here." The teasing grin the rancher tossed at him made Tad smile in return.

"I reckon I rode out here because I wanted to see if the sheriff had mentioned anything to you about his interest in Posey Jacobs."

Thane's brow wrinkled and he glared at Tad. "Posey Jacobs? No, not at all. What makes you ask that?"

"Oh, I've just noticed they've been particularly friendly of late and wanted to make sure Tully has honorable intentions where she's concerned. You know how some men are, thinking things about widows that aren't proper in the least."

Thane snorted. "The last person you have to worry about messing with Posey is Tully. If they seem chummy, there must be a reason for it, but I can assure you, Palmer, Tully wouldn't ever hurt her. It's not in his nature to do anything like that. If you step back and look at things objectively, I think you know what I say is true."

Tad nodded. What Thane said wasn't anything he didn't already know, but it didn't change the fact that he still didn't like the idea of any man spending time with Posey. Any man except him.

Aware that he couldn't push her away and simultaneously hold her close, Tad realized he needed to make up his mind.

Did he love Posey enough to let go of his doubts and fears? Did she love him enough to open her heart to loving again?

Assaulted with questions for which he had no answers, Tad helped Thane put away his tools and followed the man outside into the bright spring sunshine.

"We've sure had some nice weather recently. We're probably due for some rain, but for now, I'm not complaining about all these sunny days. It's sure made it easy to get all our spring work done." Thane looked over at Tad. "You think you might like to join us for supper? Sam will be ready to dish it up soon. We'd be happy to have you pull up a seat at the table."

Tad nodded. "Thank you, Thane. I skipped lunch and appreciate the offer. Sam always puts out a good spread."

"That he does. Come on, let's get washed up." Thane motioned for Tad to accompany him to the washstand located outside the bunkhouse where they washed their hands and faces before going inside the bunkhouse.

An older man glanced at them with a grin as he stirred something on the stove. "Well, Palmer. What brings you all the way out to the ranch?"

"Nothing in particular. Just needed some fresh air and sunshine today," Tad said, taking a stack of plates and moving to set them on the table without being asked. He'd eaten at the bunkhouse enough to know how things were done.

Thane set out cutlery then filled glasses with water. Tad helped place them on the table.

"Reckon by the time we ring the bell and the boys troop in, the grub'll be ready to eat," Sam said as he dropped hot biscuits into a basket.

Thane stepped outside and clanged a metal bar against an iron triangle. The sound carried out over his vast acres, alerting his hired men that it was time to eat.

Tad helped Sam set bowls and platters on the table. By the time the first cowboy moseyed in the door, the meal was ready and waiting.

As the men took seats at the table, they all greeted Tad with a warm word of welcome. After Thane asked a blessing on the meal, friendly conversation and lighthearted banter flowed around the table.

One cheeky young cowboy named Ben told a funny story of watching Joe Lambery get run out of a saloon in town.

"And just what were you doing at the saloon?" Thane asked the young man. Tad thought the cowboy barely looked old enough to shave but he knew he was a hard worker, and a good man.

"Now, boss, I wasn't at the saloon. I was walking by on my way to drop off that beef you sent to Tully and Maggie." Ben grinned at Thane. "You've already threatened death and destruction if you ever catch me at one again. I don't need to test your patience more than necessary."

"Again?" Tad asked with a teasing smile.

"Well, I might have gone once, just to see what all the fuss was about." Ben smirked at his employer. "Thane found out and about skinned me alive."

"I did no such thing," Thane said, pointing his fork at Ben.

"Nah, you didn't, but you sure reamed my ears about the evils of saloons and the folks who frequent them."

"Every word I said is true and you'd best not forget it." Thane gave the cowboy a knowing look then turned back to Tad. "Tully told me about his new saddle. Think you'll have time to work on a new set of reins for me?"

"Sure, Thane. Just stop by the shop next time you're in town and I can write up your order."

Two hours later, Tad swung into the saddle to head home, feeling marginally better. It had done him good to get away from town and his work, to spend time with friends.

Thane gave him an observant look and a cocky smile. "Next time you need some sunshine and fresh air, you might try riding over to Posey Jacobs' place. I've got a feeling you'd go home with a much bigger smile on your face after visiting her and Nate."

Tad ignored his teasing. "Thanks for supper, Thane. I appreciate it."

"Anytime, Palmer. Don't be a stranger."

Tad rode back to town, mulling over his options, thinking about what the pastor shared, what Thane hinted at. Dare he admit his feelings to Posey? Could he accept the gift of her love, if she was willing to offer it? Would confessing his love destroy the friendship they'd shared for years?

No closer to knowing the answers, Tad went home and spent a long, restless night of indecision. One thing was certain, though. He couldn't keep on like this. He either needed to tell Posey the truth or renew his resolve to spend his life alone.

Chapter Eleven

"Palmer, you here?"

Tad set aside the tools in his hands and wiped his hands on a rag. Due to the warm day, he'd left the door open. While it allowed air to circulate in his store, it also left him without a bell to alert him to a customer.

"Coming!" he called as he hurried to the front of the store. Frank Miller, owner of the mercantile stood in the doorway, holding a small trunk in his hands.

"What have you got there, Miller?" Tad asked as he strode to the front of the store, offering the man a friendly smile.

"I was picking up an order at the depot and this came in for you. I figured it was just as easy for me to drop this off since I was passing right by your shop."

Tad took the trunk from him and set it on the counter then gave the man's hand a grateful shake. "Thank you for doing that. I appreciate it."

"You're welcome. How's business going?" Mr. Miller asked, looking around Tad's store.

"Good. It seems like business is steady, so I can't complain." Tad grinned. "How about you?"

"We stay busy and that's the way I like it," Mr. Miller smiled. "It helps that some of the farm women are starting to bring in early produce to sell. Just yesterday, we got several baskets of fresh strawberries."

"You don't say." Tad's mouth watered, thinking about the ruby-toned summer fruit. "You have any berries left?"

"There are a few baskets of them."

Tad took money from his pocket and dropped a few coins in Mr. Miller's hand. "Save one for me? I'll come by to pick it up later."

Mr. Miller nodded. "I can do that. If you'd rather, I could send the delivery boy over with it."

"No, I'll stop by, but thanks for offering. And thanks again for bringing this delivery." Tad walked the man out the door then turned back to the counter and the trunk. He wasn't expecting any orders, so curiosity drove him as he unhooked the buckles and unlatched the clasps.

A familiar scent, one he knew well from his childhood, wafted around him as he lifted the lid and stared at a beautiful quilt. An envelope on top bore his name, written in a feathery script.

Tad tore open the envelope and unfolded a sheet of expensive parchment, embossed with his mother's initials in one corner.

Darling Theodore,

Tad cringed at her use of his full name. He'd always preferred Tad to Theodore. She was fully aware of the fact and continued to ignore it, declaring Tad to be a crude and undignified name.

Your sister sent a letter the other day. She and Colin are enjoying their trip around Europe. I would never have imagined our dear girl performing in some of the places she's visited, but she seems truly happy, and that is the most important thing.

Filled with disdain, he snorted. He'd like to know when his mother had suddenly taken an interest in his or Gloria's happiness. The woman had spent too many years focused on what pleased society in general and her snooty friends in particular.

In her letter, Gloria reminded me to send you the quilt your Grandmother Mary made for you. Although we've all nearly lost hope that you will settle down and find a wife, Gloria thinks you should have the quilt, regardless. You'll find a note from your grandmother included, too.

Tad dug around in the trunk and found a letter written in his grandmother's hand. Just seeing it made him smile and think of fun times he'd spent with the older woman. Although she'd married his grandfather when his father was a young boy, she'd treated him and Gloria as she did the rest of her grandchildren, with a great deal of love and affection.

In fact, Tad viewed her other grandchildren as his cousins. Although they were scattered across the country, he did try to keep track of where they were located.

Grandma Mary's quilts had been something that brought her great joy. He recalled watching her fingers push the needle through the fabric and batting, creating beauty from simple pieces of cloth. Posey and his grandmother had much in common and would, in fact, get along quite famously were they ever to meet.

Forcefully shifting his thoughts away from Posey, Tad returned to his mother's note.

Your father and I were so pleased to see you when you came home for Gloria's wedding. Thank you for joining us. Despite what you might think, your father and I only want what is best for you. Life there in the wilds of Oregon does seem to agree with you, son. We're happy you enjoy your life there, although I do hope you'll visit once in a while.

"Not likely," Tad mumbled and shook his head.

Please be well, be safe, and know you are loved. Take care, Theodore.
With love,
Mother

Tad set aside the letter from his mother then opened the one from Grandma Mary. He smiled as he read her brief note, telling him the quilt was for him and his bride to share on their marriage bed. She described the pattern she'd chosen for him and the reason why.

After reading what his grandmother wrote, Tad took the two letters to the back room and set them on his worktable.

Determined to see through his sudden plan, he opened a drawer and removed a small paper-wrapped package and stuffed it into his pocket. He grabbed his hat, slapped it on his head, and locked the back door. In a rush, he returned to the front of his shop and lifted the trunk. He carried it outside then locked the door behind him.

Haste lent speed to his steps as he covered the ground to Miller's Mercantile and picked up the basket of berries he'd paid for, along with a box of chocolates. Rather than make time to saddle Licorice or hitch a team to his wagon, he rushed out of town on foot, intent on reaching Posey's place.

When he arrived, he stood on the porch and tapped on the door. Footsteps echoed across the wooden floor then Posey was there, pulling the door open wide with a welcoming smile.

"Well, Tad, what brings you out here today?" she asked, moving aside so he could enter.

"Mr. Miller had some nice berries at the store. I thought you and Nate might enjoy them." He set the trunk down on the floor by Posey's sofa and then handed her the basket of berries.

She snitched one off the top and bit into it. Eyes closed in heavenly enjoyment, she savored the bite before glancing to Tad.

Heat churned in his gut as she took another bite of the berry, juice clinging to her rosy lip. It took every ounce of restraint he possessed to keep from wrapping her in his arms and kissing away that drop of berry juice from her entrancing mouth.

"They are good berries, Tad. Did you try one?"

He shook his head.

"Then you must," she said, taking a big berry from the basket and holding it out to him. When he didn't immediately take a bite, she stepped closer and rubbed the fruit across his bottom lip. "Try it, Tad."

He took a bite, wondering if she had any idea what she did to him, how crazy she made him with longing for her. If she had even an inkling of thought as to the effect she had on him, she wouldn't tempt him so.

She set the basket of berries to the side and lifted her eyebrow as he handed her the chocolates.

"It isn't my birthday or Christmas. To what do I owe the pleasure of this candy?" she asked, opening the lid and holding it out to him. He shook his head and watched as she selected a piece and took a dainty bite. "Oh, my gracious. That is so good."

She licked her upper lip and Tad bit back a groan. As though she sensed his misery, she slid closer to him. "Are you sure you don't want a bite?"

The coquettish look she tossed at him made his heart trip in his chest while his temperature began a steady climb. Rather than give in to his desire to kiss her senseless, he took the parcel from his pocket, placing it in her hand.

She glanced from it to him. "Tad? What's this? The berries and candy are such welcome, wonderful gifts, I don't need anything else."

He grinned. "You do need this. Go on. Open it."

Posey folded back the paper to reveal a small heart-shaped sewing case crafted of leather. She opened it to find a variety of needles, thread, and a tiny pair of silver scissors inside.

"Oh, Tad. It's lovely." She shot him a pleased smile. "Did you make this?"

"I did, Posey." He swallowed hard and forged ahead. "I wanted you to be able to hold my heart in your hand."

A lone tear trailed down her cheek and her fingers caressed the soft leather of the heart. "That is the sweetest thing anyone has ever said to me, Tad Palmer. I'll treasure it always. If I didn't know better, I'd think that you meant…"

Before she could finish her thought, he opened the trunk and held it out to her.

"Oh, my. It's beautiful, Tad. Absolutely beautiful!" Posey set the heart on a side table, wiped her hands on her apron, then gingerly lifted the quilt from the trunk. She spread it out over the sofa and bent down to admire the intricately stitched pattern. Curious, she looked over her shoulder at him. "Where did you get this?"

"It's a gift from my grandmother. My mother finally got around to shipping it to me, at Gloria's suggestion, of course."

Posey turned her attention back to the dusty pink roses encircled with green vines on a background of cream. "Regardless of how you came to have it, it's a lovely quilt. Rose of Sharon is a popular pattern for brides. The design stands for romantic love."

"That's what Grandma said in her note. She said that quilt is supposed to grace the bed I share with my wife."

At the word wife, Posey straightened and glowered at him, as though something he said upset or disturbed her.

"Do you have someone in mind to fill that position?" Her tone was clipped as she spoke.

"As a matter of fact, I do." Tad set down the empty trunk and took a step closer to her. "It's taken me a while to realize I can't live without her, but I hope when I ask, she'll agree to be mine."

"Oh, I see." Posey dropped her gaze and began to fold the quilt.

Tad took it from her hands and wrapped it around his shoulders, despite the sweltering heat of the day. Before she could move away, before she could protest, he took Posey's arms in his hands and pulled her to his chest, then wrapped the quilt around them both.

"You're the only one I want to share this quilt with Posey. I've loved you for so long, but I've been afraid to tell you how I feel. And part of me feels guilty for loving you. I made a promise to John to watch over you and protect you, but I never planned to be so deeply in love with you. I didn't mean for it to happen, but it did. Sometime in the last year or so, you've become so much more than the widow of my best friend. You're the woman I love."

Tears glistened in her eyes as she looked up at him. "I love you, too, Tad. I've done everything but march up and down the street with a band in front of your shop to get your attention. Despite the lingering guilt I have about falling in love again, I think John would be pleased that the man who claimed my heart is you."

He chuckled and kissed the top of her head, pulling her closer against him. "I thought you had a thing for Sheriff Barrett."

"What?" Posey pulled back and stared at him. "Why would you think such a ridiculous thing?"

"A few weeks ago, I saw the two of you having lunch at the hotel. The two of you seemed to be enjoying the time together so much, I just assumed..."

Posey rolled her eyes and sighed. "You are such a lunkhead, Tad Palmer. If you'd waited a moment, you would have seen Maggie and Nate were there, too. I was visiting Maggie when Tully stopped by to visit and insisted on taking us all out to lunch. Nate wanted to look at a gold nugget that was on display in the hotel lobby, so Maggie took him to see it while Tully and I remained at the table to place our orders. That's what you saw. Is that why you've avoided Nate and me so much lately?"

Tad nodded. "I'm an idiot, Posey, and I'm sorry I haven't spent time with either of you recently. But when I received Grandma's quilt today, I knew I couldn't avoid my feelings for you any longer. I want you to have this quilt. I want it to cover our bed and be a symbol of the love we'll share over the years. Will you please marry me, Posey Jo?"

"I will, Tad. I absolutely will!" Her arms wrapped around his neck and their mouths connected in a fiery burst of passion.

The quilt fell from their shoulders to the floor as Tad lifted her in his arms and whispered promises for the future in her ear. When Nate ran inside, trailed by Agnes and Spot, Posey didn't even bother to remind him the animals had to remain outside. Instead, she held a hand out to her son and Tad lifted the boy on one strong arm while the other encircled Posey's waist.

Nate hugged his neck and grinned. "Are you gonna be my daddy now?"

"I am," Tad said, smiling at the boy then turning to Posey again. "Just as soon as your mother decides when she'd like to wed."

"Well, don't just stand there. I'm sure Pastor Eagan would be more than happy to make us a family right now." Posey winked at Tad.

"By all means, let's go." Tad set Nate down and watched as the boy raced outside with the goat and dog trailing behind him. "We're going to be so happy, Posey. I promise. I'll never, for one single day, take for granted the special treasure I have in you. I love you both so much."

"And I love you, Tad. Today and always, with all of my heart."

Cheesy Bread

When you want to add a little zing to plain toast, this easy recipe is always a hit.

Cheesy Bread
Bread
Butter
Grated Cheese
Seasoning

Preheat oven to 350 degrees.

Butter bread and place on foil-lined baking sheet. Pop into the oven and bake for just a minute or so, until butter is melted into the bread. Remove from oven then sprinkle on a little seasoning (I like to use powdered ranch dressing mix, but an all-purpose seasoning works, too). Top that with grated cheese (you can use whatever type of cheese you like best) and return the pan to the oven. Bake about 3-5 minutes, until cheese is bubbly. Remove from oven and serve.

Thank you for reading Tad and Posey's story. If you have a moment, please review ***Tad's Treasure***. Help other readers find great new books by telling them why you enjoyed the book.

I hope we meet again on the journey to another happily ever after.

Best wishes,
Shanna

Baker City Brides Series

Crumpets and Cowpies *(Baker City Brides, Book 1)* — Rancher Thane Jordan reluctantly travels to England to settle his brother's estate only to find he's inherited much more than he could possibly have imagined.

Thimbles and Thistles *(Baker City Brides, Book 2)* — Maggie Dalton doesn't need a man, especially not one as handsome as charming as Ian MacGregor.

Corsets and Cuffs *(Baker City Brides, Book 3)* — Sheriff Tully Barrett meets his match when a pampered woman comes to town, catching his eye and capturing his heart.

Bobbins and Boots *(Baker City Brides, Book 4)* — Carefree cowboy Ben Amick ventured into town to purchase supplies… and returned home married to another man's mail-order bride.

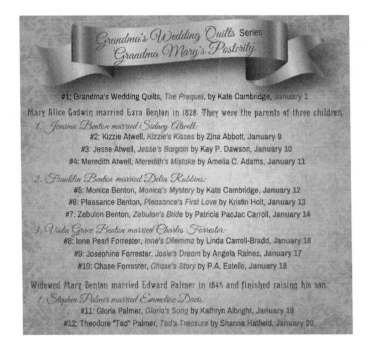

Grandma's Wedding Quilts Series
Grandma Mary's Posterity

#1: Grandma's Wedding Quilts, *The Prequel*, by Kate Cambridge, January 1

Mary Alice Godwin married Ezra Benton in 1828. They were the parents of three children.

1. Jemima Benton married Sidney Atwell:

#2: Kizzie Atwell, *Kizzie's Kisses* by Zina Abbott, January 9

#3: Jesse Atwell, *Jesse's Bargain* by Kay P. Dawson, January 10

#4: Meredith Atwell, *Meredith's Mistake* by Amelia C. Adams, January 11

2. Franklin Benton married Delia Robbins:

#5: Monica Benton, *Monica's Mystery* by Kate Cambridge, January 12

#6: Pleasance Benton, *Pleasance's First Love* by Kristin Holt, January 13

#7: Zebulon Benton, *Zebulon's Bride* by Patricia PacJac Carroll, January 14

3. Viola Grace Benton married Charles Forrester:

#8: Ione Pearl Forrester, *Ione's Dilemma* by Linda Carroll-Bradd, January 16

#9: Josephine Forrester, *Josie's Dream* by Angela Raines, January 17

#10: Chase Forrester, *Chase's Story* by P.A. Estelle, January 18

Widowed Mary Benton married Edward Palmer in 1845 and finished raising his son.

1. Stephen Palmer married Emmeline Davis:

#11: Gloria Palmer, *Gloria's Song* by Kathryn Albright, January 19

#12: Theodore "Tad" Palmer, *Tad's Treasure* by Shanna Hatfield, January 20

Grandma's Wedding Quilts-

Enjoy the romances of Grandma Mary's grandchildren. Every title is a Sweet Western Historical Romance.

You may find all twelve titles on Amazon by searching for **Grandma's Wedding Quilts**.

To learn more about our series and the individual books, visit: ***SweetAmericanaClub.com***.

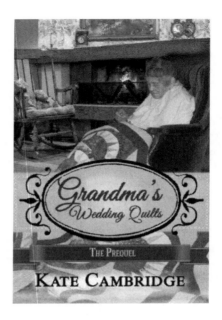

The Prequel #1 - Kate Cambridge

The greatest inspiration is often born of desperation. One year ago Hannah Quinn scored her dream job, and now the fate of the museum she loves will rise or fall on her next exhibit. But wait... there's a problem. She doesn't have a clue what her next exhibit will be!

When a trunk with two quilts is donated to the museum, Hannah's boss thinks she's wasting her time chasing down the history of the quilts, regardless of their beauty; but Hannah persists. She knows there's something special about these quilts, and a story that demands to be told.

Little does Hannah know, her friend Callum, a researcher and consultant, plays an unexpected a role in her investigation that leads to questions *and discoveries that threaten the foundation of all she holds most dear.*

Will her desperation to discover the story of the quilts cause her to lose the very thing she loves the most - or will the secrets she uncover lead her to more than she ever dreamed?

https://KateCambridge.com

Kizzie's Kisses #2 – Zina Abbott

Running from hostile Indians attacking Salina, Kansas, feisty Kizzie Atwell runs into freighter Leander Jones traveling the Smoky Hill Trail. He is as interested in her as his stallion is in her mare. The two join forces to prevent the Fort Riley Army captain from requisitioning their prize horses for the cavalry. Will the bargain they make to save their horses lead to a more romantic bargain sealed with a kiss?

http://zinaabbott.homestead.com/

Jesse's Bargain #3 – Kay P. Dawson

Thanks to a gunfight, Cora now needs to get to Kansas, and Jesse needs a new trail cook. Left with no other choice, she joins the cattle drive headed north, with a man who isn't happy to have her along. They have miles of trail ahead of them - and a lot that can go wrong along the way.

http://www.kaypdawson.com/

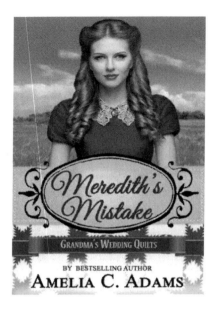

Meredith's Mistake #4 – Amelia C. Adams

The summer Meredith turned eighteen was filled with romance and laughter - two young men sought her hand, and she chose the one she thought would make her the happiest. He certainly was the most handsome, and the wealthiest, and could offer her the most pleasant life. But that turned out to be a mistake . . . one she would regret for a very long time.

In a strange twist of fate, now she's being given a chance to set things right. Will she be able to live down her past, or will her foolishness keep coming back to haunt her and keep her from ever being happy with the man she loves?

www.ameliacadams.com

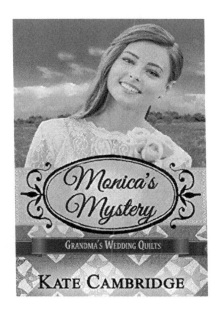

Monica's Mystery #5 - Kate Cambridge

Monica has to leave home, fast. Her parents are planning to marry her off and although all her friends are marrying, that is definitely not what she wants. She's seventeen, an amateur sleuth, and sees no reason why she can't join the ranks of the local lawman, or even become a Texas Ranger, should she choose! What will happen when she visits her best friend in Texas, only to find herself face-to-face with a handsome Texas Ranger, and knee-deep in territory she has no idea how to navigate?

https://KateCambridge.com

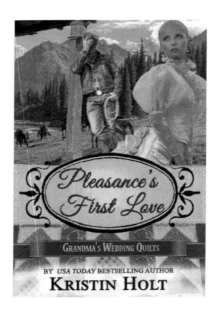

Pleasance's First Love #6 - Kristin Holt

No one will ever know how badly Pleasance Benton's abandonment threw Jacob Gideon. He landed hard, hard enough he didn't care to find a replacement. Now that he needs a woman, he figures the safest way is to order one from a catalog.

Pleasance is back to reclaim her rightful place at Jacob's side. One way or another she'll remind him theirs is a match made in heaven...once the shock wears off. The teensy-weensy problem? Jacob doesn't know that she—*his first love*—is his catalog bride.

http://www.kristinholt.com/

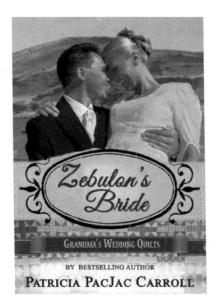

Zebulon's Bride #7 - Patricia PacJac Carroll

Zebulon Benton dreams of going to Montana, but he's the only son and his mother doesn't want him to go and his father needs help with the family store. Unknown to Zeb, his mother sends off for a mail order bride. After all, if Zeb marries and settles down, he won't want to leave.

Enter Amy Gordon from New York. She appears to be the perfect bride for Zeb. Except she also wants to go to Montana and nothing is going to stop her especially her love for Zeb.

http://www.pacjaccarroll.com/

Ione's Dilemma #8 - Linda Carroll-Bradd

Relocating from Des Moines to the Texas frontier brings more challenges than socialite Ione has ever faced. All she wants is to avoid scandal but local carpenter Morgan is intent on courtship.

www.lindacarroll-bradd.com

Josie's Dream #9 - Angela Raines

Could Doctor Josephine (Josie) Forrester and Lawman William Murphy get past their beliefs about life and love and find the future they were meant to have?

Author Page: http://amzn.to/1I0YoeL

Chase's Story #10 - P. A. Estelle

Chase wanted no part of going to college or following in his father's footsteps and becoming a Doctor. His dream involved cattle and horses and he follows that dream to the Arizona Territory. One cold, rainy day his life takes a turn when he finds himself looking down the muzzle of a Colt Walker barely being held up by a woman who has been badly beaten along with her three-year old son. Will she be someone Chase could let into his heart or someone who could destroy his life?

http://www.pennystales.com

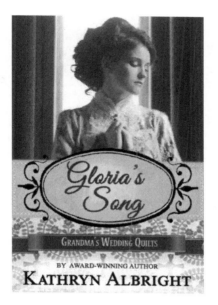

Gloria's Song - #11 - Kathryn Albright

Gloria always does the proper thing, the expected thing as the daughter of a shipping tycoon. Having, Colin, a local tavern pianist, help her with an audition is crazy. But if music can cross class lines... can it also harmonize two hearts?

Will Gloria agree to marry a man chosen by her parents, or will she find courage to shun tradition and grasp a future, insecure and thrilling, beside the man she loves.

http://www.kathrynalbright.com

Tad's Treasure #12 – Shanna Hatfield

Tad Palmer makes a promise to his dying friend to watch over the man's wife and child. Will his heart withstand the vow when he falls in love with the widow and her son?

https://shannahatfield.com

~*~

Brought to you by the authors of the
Sweet Americana Sweethearts blog.
Visit us for *sweet & clean romances set between 1820 & 1920*, including blog posts from all of us.

Author's Note

This series has been fun for me to participate in, not only because it is a great group of authors, but also because I love quilts.

Both of my grandmothers quilted, although my dad's mother was the one who always seemed to be working on a quilt project. I have two quilts she made just for me: a sweet Parasol Lady quilt from my childhood, and a beautiful Rose of Sharon quilt she made (with help from my mom) as a wedding gift when Captain Cavedweller made me his bride.

In fact, as soon as I decided to participate in Grandma's Wedding Quilts, I knew the quilt made with such love by my grandma and mother had to be on the cover of Tad's Treasure.

You'll see it there in the background, every stitch made with love.

My mom also made several quilts. Even with a busy household full of children and grandchildren, she often had a quilt frame set up in our living room during the winter months. In later years, she used a big hoop to do her quilting from the comfort of her rocking chair. Sadly, Mom can no longer see to do those tiny little stitches. Despite her best efforts to teach me, I apparently lack the gene that enables one to be a master quilter (or even a passable quilter).

But I do treasure each and every quilt we have received from family members.

Quilts are so unique and lovely and have a way of wrapping us in a warmth that goes far beyond a snuggly covering. It's more about being wrapped up in love, knowing someone went to a lot of work and effort to create something special just for us.

I hope you've enjoyed all the stories in the Grandma's Wedding Quilts series. Wishing you wonderful days ahead, hemmed with love and sweet romance.

Pendleton Petticoats Series

Set in the western town of Pendleton, Oregon, at the turn of the 20th century, each book in this series bears the name of the heroine, all brave yet very different.

Dacey (Prelude) — A conniving mother, a reluctant groom and a desperate bride make for a lively adventure full of sweet romance in this prelude to the beginning of the series.

Aundy (Book 1) — Aundy Thorsen, a stubborn mail-order bride, finds the courage to carry on when she's widowed before ever truly becoming a wife, but opening her heart to love again may be more than she can bear.

Caterina (Book 2) — Running from a man intent on marrying her, Caterina Campanelli starts a new life in Pendleton, completely unprepared for the passionate feelings stirred in her by the town's incredibly handsome deputy sheriff.

Ilsa (Book 3) — Desperate to escape her wicked aunt and an unthinkable future, Ilsa Thorsen finds herself on her sister's ranch in Pendleton. Not only are the dust and smells more than she can bear, but Tony Campanelli seems bent on making her his special project.

Marnie *(Book 4)* — Beyond all hope for a happy future, Marnie Jones struggles to deal with her roiling emotions when U.S. Marshal Lars Thorsen rides into town, tearing down the walls she's erected around her heart.

Lacy *(Book 5)* — Bound by tradition and responsibilities, Lacy has to choose between the ties that bind her to the past and the unexpected love that will carry her into the future.

Bertie *(Book 6)* — Haunted by the trauma of her past, Bertie Hawkins must open her heart to love if she has any hope for the future.

Millie *(Book 7)* — Determined to bring prohibition to town, the last thing Millie Matlock expects is to fall for the charming owner of the Second Chance Saloon.

Can forbidden love *blossom* amid the constraints of war?

"Strong characters, historical authenticity, and unique twists of fate blend with details of a wounded soldier's love."

Jane Kirkpatrick
Award-winning author of This Road We Traveled

<u>Garden of Her Heart</u> *(Hearts of the War, Book 1)* — The moment the Japanese bombed Pearl Harbor, life shifted for Miko Nishimura. Desperate to reach the Portland Assembly Center for Japanese Americans, she's kicked off the bus miles from town. Every tick of the clock pushes her closer to becoming a fugitive in the land of her birth. Exhausted, she stumbles to her grandparents' abandoned farm only to find a dying soldier sprawled across the step. Unable to leave him, she forsakes all else to keep him alive.

After crashing his plane in the Battle of the Atlantic, the doctors condemn Captain Rock Laroux to die. Determined to meet his maker beneath a blue sky at his family home, he sneaks out of the hospital. Weary and half out of his mind, he makes it as far as a produce stand he remembers from his youth. Rather than surrender to death, Rock fights a battle of the heart as he falls in love with the beautiful Japanese woman who saves his life.

A poignant, sweet romance, *Garden of Her Heart* proves love can bloom in unlikely places even under the most challenging circumstances.

ABOUT THE AUTHOR

SHANNA HATFIELD spent ten years as a newspaper journalist before moving into the field of marketing and public relations. Self-publishing the romantic stories she dreams up in her head is a perfect outlet for her lifelong love of writing, reading, and creativity. She and her husband, lovingly referred to as Captain Cavedweller, reside in the Pacific Northwest.

Shanna loves to hear from readers.
Connect with her online:
Blog: shannahatfield.com
Facebook: Shanna Hatfield's Page
Pinterest: Shanna Hatfield
Email: shanna@shannahatfield.com

If you'd like to know more about the characters in any of her books,
visit the Book Characters page on her website
or check out her **Book Boards** on Pinterest.